STRANGER ON A TRAIN

- A NOVEL -

by

Antonio F. Vianna

authorHOUSE®

AuthorHouse™
1663 Liberty Drive, Suite 200
Bloomington, IN 47403
www.authorhouse.com
Phone: 1-800-839-8640

First published by AuthorHouse 01/05/2009

ISBN: 978-1-4389-1490-9 (sc)
Library of Congress Control Number : 2008911053

Printed in the United States of America
Bloomington, Indiana

This book is printed on acid-free paper.

Chapter 1

The sudden noise of a vehicle's engine shutting off outside his house interrupts his writing. He looks through a window, just across from his desk, fingers still settled on the computer keys, to see a white mail delivery truck stop. The engine sputters a little before it shuts off, the consequences of putting off needed vehicle maintenance. Budget cuts and reallocation of money from one account to the next is usually a loosing proposition in the long run.

Fred Booth, the U. S. Postal Carrier, steps out into the sunny daylight, with a basket full of mail firmly gripped in his hands. He heads for a large metal mail repository where he intends to deposit individual household mail to the residents of this community. This is his last stop for the day, and he is anxious to complete the work. As he opens each household mail compartment with a special key, he hears his name called. The caller's voice is familiar to him. He continues the routine job task without looking up. He hurries to get the job done.

Paul Autore yells through the open den window, "Fred, don't leave before I give you something to mail. I'll be right there." He hurriedly grabs the most recent manuscript revision and places it into a pre-addressed envelope that has already been stamped with sufficient postage. Sealing the envelope

Antonio Vianna

with a few licks from his tongue, he clumsily moves away from his desk. He stumbles over several books lying on the floor before he reaches the front door, and then hurries his pace to meet Fred before it is too late.

Slightly out of breadth and embarrassed from his awkward moves, he gives Fred a genuine smile. "This needs to get to my publisher. I hope there is sufficient postage." He hands over to Fred the envelope who nods in silence toward an empty basket that he wants Paul to drop the envelope into. Paul knows the routine since he's been in this situation before. Always rushing to get things done, without seemingly never sufficient time to do everything right the first time. He stands along side Fred knowing there to be a verbal response from the mail carrier soon. He watches the man do his job in silence.

Fred finishes his tasks, stretches his back, and then turns to Paul. "Sure is a nice day. Hope the weekend is just as fine. Got some family plans to take the wife and kids to the beach." He ignores Paul's comments for the time being, knowing all too well their programmatic conversation. He waits for Paul to repeat the message.

"The manuscript needs to get to my publisher within five days. Do you think there's enough postage on it?"

Fred looks at the large brown envelope in the basket. "Seems to me if they stamped the envelope for you, they would know whether there is sufficient postage. Wouldn't you say?"

"Yeah, sure, but just the same, could you weigh it, just to be sure." Paul's eyes give off that sorry-look that usually gets him what he wants.

Fred smacks his lips, giving the impression that he is about to do something above the call of his duties, yet both men know the truth of the matter. He carries in his vehicle a postage scale with extra stamps for these precise situations. There seems to be a stare-off for a short time, each man unwilling to blink before the other one does. Paul wins out as Fred reaches for the envelope to place on the scale. He looks at the results. "Seems to be just right. No worry."

Paul takes a deep breath satisfied he's done his part.

"Got some mail for you today," Fred says as he hands over to Paul a few pieces. He takes a deep breath, not interested in continuing the conversation. He's too much focused on clocking-out to end the day, contrary to Paul, who seems interested in furthering their chat. Writing, at times, is often a solitude activity, devoid of much human contact for long periods of time. It is at these opportune moments that can break up the seclusion.

"So, you've got plans for the beach with your family." The thought of spending time with a family gives him pause to wonder what his life might have been like if he had taken the plunge into marriage. There were certainly enough occasions to do that, yet, for some reason, he always seemed to back away. His inner thoughts temporarily suspend what he was previously trying to do, to engage in some form of talk.

Picking up on Paul's brief hesitation, Fred steps aside to get into the vehicle, hoping the move to be sufficient as a final recess until the next time they meet. It works as he starts the vehicle's engine, breaking the awkward moment.

Paul blinks, involuntarily shutting and opening his eyes, to notice that his partner in the conversation is no longer standing in front of him. He turns his head to find Fred behind the steering wheel.

"Have a good weekend." Fred lifts his chin to give the final signal that he is taking off.

Paul now stands alone, holding the few pieces of mail in his hand. Once the vehicle is out of sight, he slowly shifts his eyes towards the envelopes to determine their relative importance, not suspecting to find anything of value other than second notices for unpaid bills. His initial suspicion is confirmed when he sees two pieces of urgent mail marked as *Second Notice for Unpaid Bill,* and some junk mail. He shrugs his shoulders. However, another envelope raises his interest. It is handwritten. He hesitates for a short time before he carefully opens the envelope, frowning all the time. He begins to read its contents.

Marcus Varro
2763518 West Gulf Drive
Sanibel Island, Florida 33957

Paul Autore
6511 Avenida Encinas
Carlsbad, California 92009
Dear Paul:

It has been one year, give or take a few weeks on either end, that I met you on the rail platform. You were traversing to teach a writing class in San Diego while I was finishing up a short holiday for some R&R. You might not recall me, but I am an architect, now living in Florida. Since the platform was void of other passengers and an official guardsman, I enquired of you if I was on the fitting side for my journey, and upon your affirmation, we began a pleasing conversation. We spoke of many interesting matters.

I vividly remember our exchanges since I

Antonio Vianna

found you to be a heightened listener, something
that is quite rare these days. I also recollect our
dialogue to be quite pleasantly stimulating since
one does not often make someone's acquaintance
who is a mystery writer every day. I call
this citulating, one of my word concoctions, to
elucidate when I discover something new while
traveling.

I write you to satisfy a persistent thought
that I intended to conclude some short time
after we left company of one another. I have
purchased one of your mystery novels, the one
of the distressed ghost in the projection room,
Uncovered Secrets. From the book's
narrative of this spirit, and from our brief but
intriguing conversation, I wonder if perhaps
the ghost's expressions are not somehow creeping
around within the author himself. Do you
agree or disagree that we pay for our sins in the
present life, as with Dorian Gray, or in the
future life?

Finally, I wonder if you might consider a

business opportunity from me. My daughter, who has been home-schooled from the very beginning, needs some professional guidance in reading and writing. My wife Elizabeth and I have not performed this part of our obligation to our child well enough, and thus, I wonder if you might consider being Anne's personal tutor, for, say, a few months. I assure you the financial reward would be significant, and you would have generous time to continue with your writing projects. My home is liberally large enough to satisfy a personal and private room. Please, at your earliest convenience, tell me your answer. I have no telephone availability, so a priority mail response is most suitable.

Regardless whether we shall meet up again, I truly took pleasure in our chance encounter. You are welcome to my modest accommodations at any time.

Sincerely,

Marcus Varro

Paul stares at the words in the letter, puzzled on several accounts.

"No telephone? Strange during these times. No landline is understandable, but not a cell phone. Hmm." He frowns, and then moves on to another quandary.

The next most obvious to him is the unusual mixture of formalized writing style that he ascribes to the seventeenth century or perhaps earlier along with a more contemporary style. Strange, he wonders to himself, why Marcus Varro chose these particular forms.

Next, while he slightly remembers meeting the stranger on the train, his recollection of the specifics of their conversation is sub par to that of the man from Florida. He is not sure why that might be. Might the very nature of an architect's core qualities smooth the progress of recollecting minute facts that other professionals do not possess? Or, might there be more to it? He is not sure, so he shifts his thoughts to the next area of bewilderment, the business proposition offered by the man.

It sounds interesting, and further, he could use the extra money, as made clear by the two second notices in hand. Writing isn't called a noble profession casually. He wonders what specific financial arrangement Marcus has in mind. Further, he is unsure the level of effort required to tutor his daughter and if he is up to it. He's never tutored anyone before, so he questions if he has the patience for the assignment, and, upon further contemplation, if the daughter has the willingness, desire, and motivation to learn from him.

Stranger on a Train

Lastly, he can't remember what the man looked like, young or old, tall or short, or what his voice sounded like back then. He's typically observant about the physical characteristics of people and the sound of their voices, but not this time.

There are no ready made answers to his doubts, so he decides to table the decision for a little while. A sense of urgency appears sooner than he expects.

Two weeks later Paul receives another letter from Marcus Varro.

Marcus Varro
2763518 West Gulf Drive
Sanibel Island, Florida 33957

Paul Autore
6511 Avenida Encinas
Carlsbad, California 92009

Dear Paul:

I hope this dispatch finds you well. Since I have not received any communication from

Antonio Vianna

you I write to encourage you to consider my offer of tutoring my daughter, Anne, since I feel as if I am under an enormous degree of pressure to finalize the offer. Regrettably, I told my lovely wife Elizabeth and daughter that I had arranged for Anne to be schooled by a professional author. I even offered your name to both of them and showed them one of your photos that I found on the Internet from a recent book signing. I have never seen both my wife and my daughter so excited about learning from you. I cannot disappoint them, in spite of my hasty conclusion, so I entreat for an affirmative response. Enclosed is a first class airline ticket to Fort Myers where I will meet you outside baggage claim and a financial advance on your services as a good faith effort on my part. If I appear to be desperate, I am. I look forward to having you part of my family.

Sincerely,

Marcus Varro

Believing as if a tiny situation has now grown into a gargantuan state, Paul feels overwhelmed with a mixture of confusion and anger. "What the hell does he think he is doing?" He throws the letter on the floor and walks away to simmer down. While he is not known for his emotional outbursts, he accepts his behavior as all right. He starts pacing back and forth to figure things out. Minutes later he stops the walking movement to settle on an answer. He decides to pack his bags. He arranges for his house to be looked after while he is gone, anticipating the timeline to be no more than two months, and asks a neighbor to forward his mail to the Varro address.

"Marcus, have you gone mad?" Elizabeth Varro is not pleased with her husband's decision. Her black eyes widen. "No one has been invited into this house since ...." She leaves the sentence dangling for a short time. "Have you forgotten?"

Marcus does his best to stare her down for a few seconds, but quickly realizes he is no match for her. He turns the other way. Her response is not a surprise. He had already figured out how he would counter. "No, I have not forgotten about Damien. He was my son too." His eyes flare.

She shifts away from their son's situation. "What help does Anne need?"

"It seems it is you who has forgotten."

"This conversation is going nowhere. You are not making sense."

There is desperation in Elizabeth's eyes, tension rising in an almost endless crescendo. One shoe has been dropped, now she waits for the next. "What else haven't you told me?"

He turns away as if to conceal secrets that hide in misty corners of unused rooms. She won't let the standoff pass by.

"Why didn't you discuss this with me before you invited him?"

"Simple. You would have said no, just like you are saying now."

"Simple! How can you say this is so simple? There are implications for the young man once he arrives. Have you told him everything?"

"I know there are implications. I am well aware of those. I don't need you to lecture me on that."

"Does the young man know?"

"No he doesn't. And, his name is Paul Autore. We should get use to calling him by his name."

She shakes her head in disbelief knowing the conversation will not lead to changing anything. Yet, she feels good that she has taken a stand on the matter, and will use it again once her husband's plan fails. She is convinced it will. She'll rub his nose in the dirt. "What about Anne? Does she know?"

"What do you think?"

"I'm asking you. Tell me, does she know?"

He gives her a grin that can only be interpreted as a no answer.

The silent response further infuriates his wife. She raises her hands high over her head in agony. A quiet yell sweeps through the room to no one's ears.

There is a deep stillness that cuts between them that lasts for only a few seconds but feels almost like eternity.

"What don't I know?"

Another female voice breaks the quiet. Anne Varro stands at the entrance of the door. "What don't I know," she asks again, alternatively looking between her father and mother.

No one immediately replies, waiting for the other to take the lead.

"Your father has invited someone to our home." The tone is flat and without expression this time around. Elizabeth turns her stare towards Marcus.

"Oh, that's wonderful. Tell me all about the guest." The words are said in quick order, full of excitement and hope.

"What do you mean it's wonderful? Have you too forgotten?" Her mother reloads the previous stare directed at her husband, now for her daughter.

"I'm doing it for you. Your mother doesn't seem to understand," Marcus chimes in to save his daughter from the verbal onslaught. He fondly stares at his beautiful adopted daughter. He's sure she doesn't know anything about her true self, yet he wonders how long it will be before she figures it out, assuming she hasn't yet.

"For her, or is it for you?" Elizabeth interrupts sensing she is progressively loosing the confrontation. Two against one.

Marcus squints his eyes, showing furrows on his forehead. "What do you mean, for me?"

Antonio Vianna

Elizabeth has a few more rounds left in the match, so she persists. "I think you know exactly what I mean. Why would you invite someone to this house for Anne? What on this earth does she need that you and I have not already given her?"

Anne, for the first time seems to be willing to listen to her mother's point of view. Both women shift their looks toward him waiting for an answer. Nothing comes forth. Silence, as if there are things known but cannot be said. No sound, just the strangeness that they feel that surrounds the house. Is the fear of what is known but not said only for children, or is it also for the insecure? Do ghosts of the past inflict fear in the present?

Marcus Varro walks out of the room, wordless.

"Mother, what is this all about? I really don't understand. Please tell me." She knows more than she lets on. Regularly she does her best to suppress inner demons and desires. How much longer can she hold out? She isn't sure, but suspects it's only a matter of time. She fumbles with the silver crucifix around her neck as if her mortal life depends on it.

Elizabeth looks deeply into her daughter's eyes, seeing a plea for an answer that she is not yet prepared to give. Call it a mother's way of protecting her child from unnecessary troubles, or is there more to it? Is there something so terrible that Elizabeth cannot garner enough strength or courage to tell?

Stranger on a Train

Two days later Marcus pulls his late model Porsche 911 Targa out of the carport headed for Southwest Florida International Airport in Lee County. His drive to the Airport is uneventful, making it in sufficient time to wait for Paul Autore to pick up his bags and meet him outside baggage claim.

Now standing on the sidewalk Paul feels the combination of increased temperature and humidity that is not typical of his hometown of Carlsbad, California. A prickly sensation creeps over his skin as some beads of perspiration start to accumulate on his forehead. He wipes off the moisture with the back of his hand. He scans the immediate area hoping his host will identify himself. He does not need to wait very long. He spots a man whom he now recognizes as Marcus Varro step out of an old model red color Porsche. Paul walks in the direction and soon the two men are face to face. Marcus is the first to speak.

"Welcome to Florida. I hope your flight went well." Marcus smiles and extends his hand that is reciprocated by Paul.

"Yes, everything went well."

The two men stare at each other for a few seconds that Paul feels is awkward for some reason, so he releases his grip to signal the cordial greeting has ended. Marcus picks up on the message and says, "Let me help you with your bags so we can be on our way. The drive is not very long, but without air conditioning in my car, we should try to hurry to Sanibel before the temperature rises too much. It can get terribly hot by midday."

Antonio Vianna

For some reason, Paul notices the man's speech pattern does not match his writing style, but puts that aside as quickly as the observation appeared. Soon, they are on their way. However, with the convertible top down, the hot humid air currents blow into the car minimizing much of a conversation between the two men. Paul has a few questions to ask Marcus, but figures they can wait until they reach their final destination. The trip, however, includes an unexpected turn of events.

Now off of Daniels Parkway and on McGregor Boulevard headed towards Summerlin Road, Marcus makes an attempt to say something. "Up ahead we'll be on the Causeway Boulevard that links the mainland to the island. It's rather a spectacular sight."

"I see," Paul says wondering the importance of that tiny piece of information. In spite of the open air blowing over him, he feels quite uncomfortable in the tropical climate, hoping the house is air conditioned.

Their quiet journey continues for a few more miles with the road to the Sanibel residence taking a few unexpected twists and turns due to construction, just as the future will soon be revealed. On a downhill stretch, Marcus downshifts to a lower gear. The car makes a strange sound that is not picked up by Paul. Marcus senses something isn't right so he gently presses the brake pedal. There is no response. The car accelerates in disobedience to the driver's command.

Marcus gives it another try, pushing and releasing the brake pedal alternatively in hope of finding some sort of help, but is denied again. The car advances even faster now with Marcus' hands tightly holding onto the steering wheel, not sure what his next move might be. He resists giving Paul a glance, but the frightened look on his face does not go unnoticed by the passenger.

"What's the matter?" Paul yells, eyes now widened realizing something is not right.

Marcus remains quiet. He does not have an answer. With slower traffic on each side of him, he tries to zigzag to avoid a collision, but just ahead spots a large truck moving much slower than the rest of the vehicles. He believes he has only one option, so he quickly swerves onto the edge of the road. The Porsche finds a final resting place along the roadside barely missing nearby construction workers. No one seems to be injured. Both men sit quietly in the car, consumed of shock, yet thankful of still being alive.

Within moments nearby workers rush to their side and call for emergency help. Marcus and Paul are driven to a nearby hospital and later released with only minor cuts and bruises. "You're both lucky to be alive. Your seat belts probably saved you from being thrown from the car. Here is some medication should you feel any further pain or discomfort. Check with your primary care physician as a follow up." The emergency physician hands each of them a prescription and then leaves the two men alone, needing to attend to other patients requiring more urgent care.

"Welcome to Sanibel," Marcus says to Paul with a bit of a chuckle.

The unexpected comment is just enough to break the tension. "Is this how all guests are welcomed?" Paul tries to one-up his host.

"We don't get many visitors to the house."

"I think I know why." Paul flicks his eyebrows.

Silence for a short time.

With unusual calmness, Marcus says, "Let's get out of here. We need to find a car rental company. I hope you have a driver's license handy because I don't. Left it at the house. You'll need to be on record for the loaner. I'll pay for it."

While he says it as more of a directive than a request, Paul does not question it. If fact, he is somewhat relieved that he'll be driving the vehicle and not the other way around. "What are we waiting for? Let's make the phone call."

It is a time like this, when people go through an emotional or physical challenge together, that brings them together. And so it is with Marcus and Paul. A sort of bond has developed between them, but will be challenged later on. Will their relationship be strengthened or will cracks develop to threaten their tie to each other?

During the final leg of the trip to the Sanibel residence Paul drives a new Chevrolet Impala, air conditioned. He turns to the passenger, "How are you feeling?"

Marcus is silent for a moment, seemingly thinking about something he wishes for the time being to keep to himself. Then he says, "Huh?"

"I said, how are you feeling? That was a pretty scary thing we just went through. I'm still shook up over it, but you seem pretty calm."

"Oh, I'm just thinking how lucky we were. I mean, it could have been worse." He looks through the passenger side window to nothing in particular, still thinking of those private thoughts.

"What do you think happened?"

"Huh?"

"I said, what do you think happened back there? Your brakes gave out is my best guess. What do you think?"

"I recently had the entire car in for a check up. Everything was working fine just a few weeks ago. I don't know what happened, really."

"But your brakes gave way. At least, that's what it seemed like to me."

"Yeah, that's what it seemed like to me as well."

"Your insurance company will surely figure it out. Don't you think?"

"No, I don't think so."

Paul quickly glances towards Marcus, "Say again?"

"I don't think so."

"Why? I mean that's what insurance companies do before they settle a claim. They investigate what went wrong. Unless, you have some new type of insurance company that the rest of us don't have."

"I don't have an insurance company. I'm not insured with an insurance company. I'm self-insured. I don't trust them."

"Oh."

"I've already informed a towing company to take the Porsche to someone I trust to determine the cause of the problem. Then, I'll get it repaired."

Antonio Vianna

"Oh."

"Don't be so surprised. I'm not your average person, neither is my family. You'll see."

"What is that suppose to mean?" Paul now feels a lump develop in his throat, something that signals a warning sign ahead. He takes a deep swallow.

"Nothing to be frightened about. We're just a little different than most people you know. Don't worry, you're in no danger."

"Why should I worry about being in danger? I thought you wanted your daughter to be tutored. I mean, that's what I signed up for, to tutor your daughter." His voice now shows sign of some strain.

Marcus shifts his glance away from the side window to look forward. A grin appears on his face. "Yes, and that is exactly what I want you to do, to tutor my lovely daughter, Anne." He then turns slightly to look at Paul to see his facial expression of worry.

In spite of the comfortable temperature within the air conditioned automobile, Paul beings to perspire. He wonders what he has gotten himself into. On the surface, it seemed to be just a normal tutorship, but is there something lurking beneath the façade of serenity that not even Paul can envision?

"We've been through a near death experience together, Paul. You simply need to trust me."

The turmoil Paul feels is not lessened with those remarks.

As if the conversation had not taken place, Marcus says, "Once we cross over the Causeway Bridge, take a right on

Periwinkle Way, then after a short distance, take a left on Rabbit, and then a right on West Gulf Drive. We're almost there. I'll take the lead in explaining why we are not in the Porsche."

Paul does not hear a word that is said, too much consumed by a creeping fear of the unknown.

Twenty minutes or so later, Paul pulls up to 2763518 West Gulf Drive. The place looks like a white mansion to him. He gapes in awe without self-control. Marcus is the first to leave the vehicle, showing a slight limp that might be from tightening of muscles caused from the car mishap and the long sedentary drive. He thinks about asking him about it, but is interrupted from further thought when Marcus motions him to come along.

Paul steps out of the Impala and finds stiffening in his legs and back, confirming for the time being the same causation on both men. "Let me help you with your bags," offers Marcus now standing in front of the car waiting for a response.

"Here, take this. I'll grab the larger one."

Now, both men arrive at the front door simultaneously. Before Marcus can open it, someone from inside gets there first. Standing in the open door space is Anne, a specimen of beauty to Paul's eyes. He remains motionless until she breaks the silence.

"Father, what took you so long? Mother and I worried that something terrible might have happened." She remains fixed on her father, now stepping aside to let him walk through the door opening. When there is no immediate response she turns to Paul. "You must be Paul Autore, my tutor. Welcome." She gives him one of her best smiles that start to melt him into a watery-like substance.

Now a few feet away Marcus chimes in, "Come this way Paul. You'll have more than enough time to get acquainted with your pupil. There is someone else you need to meet."

Paul had figured Anne would be much younger. What possibly could he teach this young woman, he asks himself privately?

Anne shrugs her shoulders and puckers her lips, both of which tingles Paul's attraction to the young woman.

"Elizabeth, please join me in the living room. Our guest has arrived."

His wife arrives shortly. She seems almost as young as her daughter, Paul thinks to himself.

"Elizabeth, this is our guest and Anne's tutor, Paul Autore. Paul, this is my lovely wife, Elizabeth."

The introductions seem quite formal and unsettling to Paul for some reason. His brain tries to process the bits of information but does not arrive at any logical end conclusion. He is embarrassed when he finds himself staring at Elizabeth's hand extended toward him. He wonders how long he has been in a self-induced trance. Quickly, he extends his hand to shake with hers, finding the grip to be stronger than he had expected. He is unsure how to further respond since he does not know exactly what she might have said. However, he is rescued by Anne in the nick of time.

"Paul must be tired from the trip and all. Perhaps we should give him a little personal quiet time."

"Yes, that is a good idea," Elizabeth says, "Why don't you show him to his room so he can unpack and rest a bit before dinner."

Paul picks up on the save, "Thanks. I am a little tired from the trip and unnerved from our recent accident. I could use a little ...."

"What accident?" asks Elizabeth. She redirects the question to her husband.

"Oh, nothing to worry about. Just a little car trouble. That's all." He tries to sooth over the previous misfortune but knows it comes up short. He'll let her in on the details later on, in private. "Now Paul, let Anne show you to your room where you can freshen up and rest before dinner. Say at ...." He now looks at his wife.

"Say at six-thirty. That should give Anne and me enough time to prepare. Is that acceptable to you, Paul?"

Now part of the conversation, he quickly answers, "Yes, that's fine with me."

"Follow me," Anne says as she walks away carrying the lighter of two luggage bags.

Just soft enough so no one can overhear, Paul says, "Anyplace you want to take me."

Now alone, Elizabeth turns to her husband. "Tell me about the misfortune. What happened?"

He moves to a nearby overstuffed chair where his wife joins him sitting nearby. "Something happened to the brakes of the Porsche."

She frowns, not clear what he means, and so she remains quiet knowing he will explain when he is ready.

"The drive seemed to go well, but on the return trip, the brakes gave out. I was going downhill and to avoid colliding with other vehicles I had to swerve off the road. The car didn't roll or anything such as that, but it sure gave me a hell of a scare. Paul too."

"No injury to you, him, or anyone else?"

"No one, just a few cuts and bruises, and now I'm feeling a little tightening in my legs and back. From the trauma, I'm sure."

She moves closer to him to hold his hand. "Do you want to rest? We can delay dinner for a while, even postpone it. I'm sure Paul must feel tired as well."

"No, let's get tonight over with. There is enough to do starting tomorrow."

"As you wish." She pauses. "I thought you had the car serviced just recently."

"I did. And that's the troubling part. Julien has always done excellent work for us. I'm having the car towed to him for a look over to determine exactly what caused the brakes to give out."

In another part of the house, Anne and Paul start to get acquainted.

Stranger on a Train

"Are you going to be as quiet as my father?"

"What do you mean?"

"What kind of accident happened?"

"Oh, that."

"Yes, that."

They stand facing each other just outside the room where Paul will stay. He sets the luggage bag on the floor. She does the same with the smaller bag.

"I think the brakes to the Porsche gave out. We were going down a hill and your father couldn't stop the car. We went off the road and wound up several feet away, down an embankment. I think we were lucky the car didn't roll or hit someone."

She frowns in a way that could be interpreted as confusion or disappointment. "No one was injured?"

"We were taken to a nearby urgent care where we were patched up. I couple of bruises for me. I think the same with your father. Nothing more. We were sure lucky."

She puckers her lips, not the appealing way he previously found them to be, but something different. He's not sure, just different. "Oh."

He doesn't know if it is his turn to say something so he waits for a second or two. She relieves him of the decision.

"Well, here is your room. I'll let you unpack and get some rest before dinner. If you need anything, just give a holler." She smiles, "Someone will come to your rescue." Then she turns and leaves Paul standing alone outside the room.

He opens the door and looks around. The room is decorated nicely, although sparsely. He sets his luggage on the floor and begins to open a few doors to find the closets, a large bathroom, and an exit to a small seating area outside. He approves and as he starts to unpack he notices a few magazines, one in particular, *Car Maintenance and Repair*. He thinks nothing of them as he sets them aside. Several minutes later he flops down on the bed and is fast asleep.

A few hours later Paul is awaken by a strange sound that he can't make out. Still a little groggy, he lifts his weary body out of bed, feeling more now than before some aches and pains in his legs and back from the previous car accident. He reminds himself to take a few tablets given by the physician. But for now, he is more interested in finding the origin of the peculiar noise. It seems to be coming from someplace in the hallway, nearby his room.

He opens the door and gently walks into the middle of the hallway to look around. The noise seems to have disappeared, yet he decides to linger a little longer before calling off his search. The wait pays off as the same sound reemerges. He thinks it is coming from inside a nearby room, so he approaches the only other door that is visible to him. Leaning his head towards the door he turns so that his right ear is flush with the wood. At first the noise is faint, almost nothing. But then, without notice, the sound reemerges. The change in volume startles him as he jumps away. Still staring at the door, he hears a clicking sound as if a lock is being turned. His heart starts to race a little. Next, he sees the door knob turn and finally the door opens about three to four inches. He remains put, not sure what he should do. That decision is made for him as the door immediately slams shut creating another eerie sound that causes him to jump back again. Now, all is quiet. He decides to call off the investigation and return to his room.

There he remains for another ten to fifteen minutes until he hears a knock on his room door. His body flinches from surprise. He manages to say, "Yes, who's there?"

"It's me, Anne. Dinner is ready. Please join us in the dinning area."

"Sure, give me a few minutes."

There is no response since she has no intention to wait for an answer. She is well on her way to dinner.

Shortly, Paul shows up and takes what appears to be a predetermined place at the dinner table. He isn't sure if he should bring up the weird noise he just recently heard along with the door opening and shutting.

"Hello Paul. Please take a seat, next to Anne," says Elizabeth. Her words sound calm and comforting.

"Did you have a good rest?" asks Anne. Her smile is brighter than when he first met her.

"Um, yes. I think, though, I might have had a little dream that interrupted my sound cat nap."

Marcus, not having said anything yet, now asks, "A little dream?" He gives his wife at quick glance that goes unnoticed by Paul. She conceals her worry, and wishes the topic to be changed without further discussion. However, Anne chimes in.

"Tell us Paul. What was the dream about?" She seems quite interested in knowing about it as she leans toward him, eyes brightly focused.

Before Paul can answer Elizabeth says, "I think that might be a little too private for someone to share with people he's just met." She takes a hasty and deep swallow. "Perhaps once he gets to know us we can ask such personal things." She scans the family members with disapproving eyes.

"Oh mother, Paul is a grown man. I think he can decide for himself." She fights off her mother's censure, but seems to lose the contest when Marcus tries to end it.

"I agree with your mother. Perhaps at a later time. Paul isn't going away just yet." The look on his face is a combination of a grin and a smirk, difficult to interpret.

Paul does not pick up on the message and decides to offer a brief explanation. "It seemed so real, the dream, that is. I mean, it could have actually happened." He does not notice the displeasure on Elizabeth's face. "I thought I was awakened by a weird sound that I had not heard before. I laid in bed for a few seconds to get my bearings, to determine if the sound was from a dream and therefore gone, or if the sound was real, and that I would hear it again."

28

"Paul, you don't have to tell us. Really." Elizabeth's comments are ignored as Paul continues, more as if he is in a trance at the moment.

"When there wasn't a sound, I figured it was all a dream. I closed my eyes to get another few minutes of comfort. But then, I heard the sound again."

Anne interrupts, "What was the sound like? Can you describe it?" She is genuinely fascinated by his recollection.

"No, I can't really describe it. I've never heard that type of sound before."

Anne persists in her questioning. "Maybe it was the sound of the Porsche crashing. You and father just had a terrible experience. Maybe you were recalling the accident?"

"No, nothing like that. This sound was weird. I'd say it was eerie to my ears."

"Oh," Anne says, putting her hand to her mouth. A pause ensues. Then she takes her hand away from her mouth to encourage him to continue. "Go on. Tell us more."

"Please Anne," Elizabeth pleads.

Paul ignores the comment. "Then, I stood up and began to walk around the room to figure out where the sound was coming from. I finally decided to open the bedroom room and step into the hallway where the sound was loudest. I looked around and noticed another door nearby, so I walked towards it."

"No." The one word defines the anguish Elizabeth feels.

Paul looks her way. "Did I say something to frighten you?"

The focus is now on Elizabeth who remains otherwise quiet. Her face is full of fright as if she just witnessed a calamity and is not able to cope with it very well. Is she acting or is it real?

"Mother, are you all right?" Anne moves close to her side, touching her hand, feeling nerves vibrate muscles.

Marcus watches, figuring he knows the root cause of his wife's reactions. He intentionally remains seated fully aware that the situation will soon pass.

Anne turns to Paul. "Perhaps we can continue this at another time." She turns to her mother. "Take a sip of water. Here."

It is Elizabeth's turn to say something. "I'm very sorry. I don't know what came over me. I'm embarrassed."

"It is me who should be sorry. I think I just got carried away. I mean, I am a writer who tells stories," says Paul who hopes to lighten up the tension. He gives off a genuine smile that seems to work for everyone.

"Ok, that's settled. Let's return to dinner. I'm famished." Marcus hopes his words are final. Then he adds, "And tomorrow, Paul and I need to talk more specifically about his next few months with us."

Along with eating the meal, the next hour or so is spent talking about tidbits of information that relate to the history of Sanibel Island. Paul finds the dialogue to resemble a sales pitch for a timeshare.

Once the meal is finished, Paul says, "I hope you will excuse me, but I am quite tired from the trip. My body doesn't respond well to time zone changes. Will you forgive me if I turn in?"

"Quite understandable," says Marcus. "Get up when you feel ready. We don't have breakfast or mid-day lunch at any specified time, just dinner. You'll find food in the kitchen, so help yourself. Elizabeth and I are early risers."

"I don't take after my parents," Anne chips in with a big smile to everyone. "They're the larks, I'm the owl." She looks at Paul, "What are you?"

"An owl," he says with great pleasure to himself realizing that he and Anne are in a similar pattern. He hopes she feels the same way, but will find out some inconsistencies in her story later on.

"Wonderful. I've found someone with whom I am in sync." She touches a silver crucifix handing around her neck.

A big smile gushes his way that gives him shivers. He feels a little flush, hoping his face is not as red as he thinks it might be.

Marcus stands, which seems to be the official signal to permit others to follow his lead. Paul tells himself to remember the formal protocol.

As Anne and Paul walk away, Marcus and Elizabeth stay put. They have something to talk about. Once out of ear's distance, Marcus turns to his wife. "What came over you this evening? Are you trying to scare him off?"

"I think you know." She hesitates a second before continuing. "The noise from behind the door … it's returned." She makes it sound quite real.

"It's never left us. But I am surprised it reappeared so soon."

"Do you think he is in danger?"

"We all are in danger at some level. You know that."

"The door is locked. No one can open it. We've cut off that part of the house so no one can go there." She continues in a serious tone.

"Yes I know. I only hope it lasts." Unlike his wife, he feels a real threat is imminent.

Once at the top of the stairs Anne turns to Paul. "What else did you dream?" She stares at him like a pupil asking her teacher an important question that will appear on her midterm.

Taken aback, he says, "Why is that important to you?"

"That's very good. Answering a question with another question," she smiles. "Very clever. Is this an example of what I am in store for?"

"Well, maybe. But I really do want to know why you're interested in my dream."

"Didn't Freud say that we live part of our life through dreaming? That we are what we dream." She frowns for a second, and then continues. "Or did he say that we dream what we are?"

"Probably both."

"Ok, then. Tell me the rest of the dream, or are you embarrassed?"

"That's a strange question. Why would I be embarrassed?"

"Come on Paul. We all dream things that we'd rather have kept private. You, me, mother, father, everyone."

He decides to shift the conversation to her. "Tell me what you've dreamt that you'd prefer be kept private?"

"Not so fast. We don't know each other well enough, at least not yet. And further, if I told you something that I prefer to be kept private, then it wouldn't be private any longer."

"But I'd keep it private between us."

"Maybe sometime later. Not now. But back to your dream. You were about to tell my entire family your dream just a little while ago, so why won't you tell me it now? Right now." She senses his hesitation so she decides to influence his decision. She touches his arm, and then squeezes it just so. "Come on Paul. You can tell me. I'm listening."

She wins the exchange. "Ok." He takes a deep breath. "As I said at the dinner table, I walked toward the door to make sure the sound was coming from that direction. I put my right ear against the door. At first there was very little sound. I could barely hear it. But then, the sound returned and got louder. The change in volume startled me so I quickly backed away. I remember staring at the door, and then I'm sure I heard a clicking sound as if the door's lock was being turned. I froze, only able to look at the door." He takes a gulp of air and then continues. "The door knob slowly turned and then the door opened about three to four inches and quickly slammed shut."

His eyes are now wide as he recounts the episode. "I hurried back to my room. And that was that."

She frowns. "That part of the house has been off limits for a while, since …." Her eyes are now focused on the floor. Was it a dream or was it something else?

"Since when?" he asks realizing there is more.

She forces a smile, "At another time." She extends her hand towards him, "Good night Paul. I'll see you tomorrow." She walks away headed to her bedroom.

There are no sounds in the house right now, yet there are angry spirits lurking in the walls, demanding admission. The emptiness seems alive with loneliness.

Chapter 2

Paul's sleep is restless, tossing and turning, thinking about what Anne said to him, about the part of the house being off limits. Further, why wouldn't she tell him the reason? He knows there is more to the story and intends to find out somehow. It must be writer's curiosity or something.

Daybreak comes sooner than he wishes. He lies in bed, trying to rub away the tension he feels in his forehead. He is not successful in removing the annoyance, so he decides to get up to start the day.

As he shaves to ready himself to make his way downstairs to get a bite to eat, he gets a feeling someone is watching him, so he looks in the bathroom mirror to determine if anyone is behind him. He sees no one, other than his own weary face from a lack of sleep covered in white shaving cream. Yet the sensation persists. He turns his entire body around. "Who's there?" He waits for a response. Nothing replies yet he is suspicious.

Antonio Vianna

Slowly he moves around, walking as if he is on egg shells, intending to keep the symbolic white colored objects whole. Then, without any warning, a noise comes and then quickly goes. It takes him by surprise. He jumps, dropping the razor onto the floor. He feels his heart take off, like a sprinter at the sound of the starting pistol. He knows he shouldn't be afraid, but he is.

He takes in a deep swallow, secretly hoping nothing more happens. His eyes roam the room finding no one and nothing. He bends over to pick up the razor when he hears another noise. This time the sound is familiar. Is someone knocking on the bedroom door? He listens for more.

"Paul. This is Anne. Are you up?"

He waits a little longer, for what, he's not sure. He just waits, figuring it to be a safe bet. He wonders why she is up so early. Didn't she tell him she is an owl, just like him?

The same voice continues. "I'm going down to breakfast. See you later."

He looks towards the door and smiles, the kind of facial expression when you believe everything is alright. He hesitates before saying something. He looks down at the floor thinking his hand is close to the razor, but is surprised when he sees there is a three feet separation. Has his hand moved, or, has the razor jumped away? He shrugs off the dilemma and settles in on reaching for the instrument. Now grasped firmly in his hand, he returns to the bathroom to finish off the shave. A few minutes later he leaves the bedroom headed downstairs for breakfast.

Stranger on a Train

Elizabeth and Anne are seated at the table, drinking coffee and eating some sort of fruit that is not at first recognizable to Paul. His appearance calls for a response from the two women. Elizabeth speaks first.

"How was your sleep?" The tone is sincere and authentic.

Paul looks at both women wondering what part of his dream and this morning's incident he should share. He decides to hold off for the time being. "Good for the most part."

"How so?" Anne asks. Her eyes are warm and kind looking. She is not convinced.

He takes in a breath of air and then moves a little closer to the table. "Well, it's just that a new bed takes some getting use to. I think I was restless after the trip and car accident."

"Makes sense. If you need to take a nap, don't let it worry you. We understand." Anne continues.

"Help yourself to coffee and juice. They're both right here." Elizabeth points to a large carafe of coffee and a pitcher of orange juice on the table.

"What's that you're eating," Paul asks Elizabeth.

"Pomegranate. Want some?"

"Looks good. Yes. Where is it?"

"I'll get it for you. Have a seat by mother," Anne says as she stands up to run the chore.

Paul takes a seat next to Elizabeth and then reaches for the coffee carafe. "Where's Marcus? I thought he'd be up and about by now. He seems to me to be an early riser."

"You are right about that."

His brow shows confusion, not sure part of what he said is right.

"He gets up very early in the morning. Leaves the house to take care of his businesses, and then returns sometime in the mid afternoon. He has many interests to manage." She rolls her eyes.

"Oh, I see."

"Do you, really?"

He is not sure how to answer the question, so he lets it drop. Anne returns in the nick of time.

"Here you go. I hope you enjoy it. It's like an orange." She places a small bowl of fruit on the table in front of him and takes her original seat.

"Perhaps after you have had your breakfast, Anne can show you the grounds and a quick tour of the house." She directs her comments to Paul, but then smiles at her daughter. "Would you mind at all in showing him around before your father returns?"

"No. That sounds like a wonderful idea." She nods approvingly at her mother, and then looks towards Paul. "We can get to know each other a little as well."

He takes it all in, figuring it to make sense.

After a few more minutes of casual chit chat, Elizabeth leaves to take care of some personal matters. Paul and Anne remain together. He fiddles with the spoon previously used to eat the pomegranate. Anne notices.

"What's on your mind?" Her voice is soft and soothing.

"Huh? What do you mean?" He clears his throat.

"I'm a bit psychic, but there's not much to worry about. I keep it mostly to myself." She pauses and then continues her comments to Paul. "You have something to say. I know." Her body is motionless. She does not take her eyes away from him.

He glances away to consider what to say next. The seconds seem to stretch out. "Psychic?"

"That's what I'm told." She patiently waits, knowing he is going to continue.

"Ok, here it is." He swallows. "I'm not real certain what I'm suppose to do here."

"Didn't father tell you?"

"Oh yes, he told me something."

"What was that?"

"That he wants me to provide you with some professional guidance on writing and reading, sort of like a tutor." He waits for her to say something but she is quiet. He continues. "He told me that you and your mother were happy that I decided to the arrangement." Again, he looks at her for some sort of response, but she remains silent. "Now all of that doesn't seem to be odd. I know that. But, well, you don't seem to be the kind of person who needs any tutoring. I mean, you just don't." He decides to wait her out for a response.

She picks up on his need to hear from her. "What kind of person do I seem to be? What does a person do to suggest she needs professional writing and reading help? Paul, quite honestly, I am the one who is confused."

"I know that sounds strange, but, it just doesn't feel right to me. I mean, the way your father contacted me. The two letters, and then the airline ticket and a financial advance. It's all too weird."

"Perhaps it's weird to you, but father is not your ordinary run of the mill person. He's, well, different than others. You've already picked up on that. I wouldn't worry about that for now."

"You wouldn't?"

"No, I wouldn't. But, I think there are other things worrying you. Tell me. You can trust me." Her soft voice and gentleness encourages him to continue.

"In addition to the situation that I talked with you about last night … you remember, the opening and closing of the door with the strange noise … I heard another bizarre sound this morning right before you knocked on my bedroom door. I got the distinct feeling that someone was watching me."

She opens her eyes wide and furrows show on her forehead.

"Now, hold on. I know what you're thinking. But Anne, I really heard something odd and yes, I did feel that someone was watching me or spying on me. Honest."

She nods her head a few times to comfort him. She wonders how much she should share with him.

"Now it is you who looks as if she wants to say something to me. Am I right? Do you want to share something with me?"

Stranger on a Train

"This house is very old. I'd say easily over a hundred years. We moved here about ten years ago. There were five of us then." She pauses to reconsider going on. "My younger brother, Damien, disappeared shortly after we moved in. Even today, we do not know where he is, or how he disappeared. We don't know if he is alive or passed on … and then … Edna … so sad…."

Paul remains silent, taking it all in and not prepared to ask any questions, at least not yet, although he has a few. He hopes she continues on. He is not disappointed.

She glances away, pausing long enough so that you know whatever she is about to say is not planned. "I started to hear strange sounds in this house right after Damien disappeared. Then mother heard them, and finally so did my father. At first none of us wanted to admit to each other any of this, but eventually I broke down. I had to. I couldn't keep it inside any longer." She purposely avoids mentioning Edna again.

He wants to extend his hand to her, to console her, to help her through the confession-like talk, but he holds back for fear he might interrupt her thoughts.

She lowers her voice as if she does not want the air in the house to pick up the conversation and carry it to a place where others could overhear. "At first, we all convinced each other the sounds were really sounds you get from an old house. You know, the creaking sound of wood, or a tree limb rubbing against the outside. We get a lot of rain in these parts at times, and when it rains, the noise seems to sound like someone crying out. It echo's off the walls and ceiling."

His face turns a little squeamish as if he just witnessed a ghoulish scene. His eyes are so large you can't see the white part.

She picks up on his reaction. "Don't get frightened on me. You asked me and I'm telling you. I can stop this anytime."

"No, don't stop. I'm just taken aback a little. I can deal with it. Go on, please."

"Are you sure?"

"Come on. What else could there be?"

She looks at him in a way that sends a shiver up his spine, yet he does not want to let on. He nods to encourage her to continue.

"Ok, then. Father is very possessive of mother and me. He wants to know everything we do, and everyone we see. We're almost like hostages in this house. And when he told us he had invited a guest to join us, we were, well both shocked and happy at the same time. We couldn't believe it. We haven't had a guest in this house since Damien disappeared."

"So you don't need any tutoring? Is that what you're telling me?"

"Well, I might need some help in writing and reading, but not to the point of requiring a tutor. No, not that at all."

"Why then did your father ask me here? What other motive might he have?"

"Paul, that's a good question both mother and I have yet to figure out."

"Maybe I should ask your father myself. That would give us the answer."

A worried look comes over her. "No, don't do that. You must never tell him or my mother that we've had this conversation. Never. You've got to promise me that. Do you promise?"

He hesitates before answering.

"Paul, you must promise me. Please." The troubled look persists, but is it real?

"Ok, you have my word on it. Cross my heart."

Paul thinks to himself that he might just have to find a way out of the situation. Nothing comes to mind now, but he swears to himself not to stay here one minute longer than he has to.

As if Anne is reading his mind she says, "Don't leave me."

He is not sure what to make of the comment. Before he can get a word out she says, "Let's change the topic. I promised mother I would show you around the grounds and give you a tour of the house. Follow me." She stands and walks away with Paul close behind as if the previous conversation had not taken place.

Elsewhere, there is another concern.

"What did you find?" His stare is a fierce combination of anger and curiosity.

"Mr. Varro, you are not going to like what I have to say."

Marcus's stare continues without a need to say anything further. His impatience grows exponentially.

"The brakes gave out. They were tampered with."

Marcus, unaccustomed to surprises, opens his mouth wide, shocked at what he is told. "How can that be?"

"I can only tell you what mechanically went wrong."

"Go on." Marcus fiercely looks at the high performance vehicle, glowering at the notion that someone would deliberately mess with the brakes.

"Your car had excellent brakes. I installed them myself and I service your vehicle on a regular schedule. You know that."

"Yes, yes. Go on. I'm not accusing you of any wrong doing. I trust you. You have been with me too long."

Julien nods, thankful that his boss does not suspect him of disloyalty. "Yet, brakes are still subject to wear." He waits for a response but Marcus is silent, so he continues. "The rate at which brakes wear out depends on how they are used. Mr. Varro, if I might comment, you muscle the brakes, stepping on them at the last second to stop. This adds to the wearing on the pads and linings."

Marcos waves his hand the way one does to brush-off the observation as not important. He puckers his lips to reinforce the hand motion.

"Further, our climate in Florida such as the hot humid weather and the salt from the ocean cause brakes in general on all vehicles to wear faster. Have you heard the brakes squeal on occasion?"

Marcus isn't sure he is being asked a question so he shrugs his shoulders without commenting.

Julien continues. "Tires also wear out faster in Florida-like conditions." He senses that his boss is anxious for him to move on. "I installed a power assisted hydraulic dual circuit brake system with disc brakes both at the front and the rear. They function independently. One circuit operates the front while the other operates the rear. If one brake circuit fails, the other will still operate, but you will notice that it takes a little longer in distance to stop the car. It seems that the rear brake circuit was completely destroyed, which is what this vehicle mostly relies on, while the front circuit was only partially destroyed. You were able to get to Ft. Myers with the use of the front brakes, but as you drove back to Sanibel, you probably were in a hurry, so you drove faster and applied the front brakes with more muscle. The front brakes just gave out under those conditions. It seems you had the top down so you could not hear any squealing of the brakes. If you had heard the noise, that might have given you a clue something was not right with the brakes."

"So you're saying somebody purposely knew about how Porsche brake system functions and planned that there would be an accident with both Paul and me in the car together! Is that what this is all coming down to?"

"Mr. Varro, all I am doing is explaining how your Porsche brake system operates and what failed. That's all. Nothing more."

"Yes, yes. I understand. But who would want to do this?" He turns his head away from the vehicle, trying to arrive at some answer. Then he turns back to face Julien.

"Can any one do this?"

Antonio Vianna

"Excuse me?"

"Can any one tamper with these brakes?"

"No, not anyone. You'd have to know how this particular system operates."

"So, it would have to be a car mechanic?"

"No, not necessarily."

"Why not? I thought you said you'd have to know this system, the Porsche brake system that you just described to me."

"Anyone who has access to Porsche maintenance manuals could figure it out. Also, there are many car maintenance and repair magazines that describe the mechanics of this. Don't forget the Internet."

"So, it could be almost anyone? Is that what you are saying?"

"Yes, Mr. Varro, that's exactly right. Anyone who can get access to procedures on building, repairing, or maintaining a brake system, like the one in your Targa, could also know how to mess it up."

"That doesn't help me much."

"I'd consider why someone would want to harm you or your new guest. My guess is your guest is the target."

"That's interesting. Why do you say that?"

"If you were the target, then the brake failure or some other mechanical failure could have been created to happen when you were driving alone. But, in my opinion, the brakes were damaged in a way that they would give out on your return trip, when you and your guest were together in the car.

But, that's just my guess. I'm not an investigator. I'm just a mechanic."

"No, no. That makes a lot of sense … a lot of sense." He pauses. "But who would want to see Paul and me dead?" He looks directly at Julien for no particular answer.

Julien swallows deeply, wondering if he is being fingered as a suspect. "I don't know." The words seem strained. Is that because Julien has something to hide, or is he just responding to the expression on his boss's face.

Marcus begins to pace back and forth, nodding his head as if he is trying to shake something out that will put the pieces together. Is the road between Ft. Myers and Sanibel full of twists and turns, just as the future will soon be revealed? Then he stops and glances towards Julien for no apparent reason. He thinks to himself that he should look backwards, not to the future, for the answer. As he walks away, he asks, "When will the Targa be repaired?"

"Give me three days if I can get the parts by tomorrow. More time if they need to be ordered."

"Stop by the house when you know for certain." He walks away, headed for the main house to check in with Paul.

Marcus finds Anne and Paul sitting in an outside area underneath an umbrella to ward off the sun's rays. A slight breeze helps cool the temperature and facilitate moisture evaporation from their skin. They sip ice tea. They seem to be two friends just enjoying a good laugh together. Anne spots her father approaching. "Looks as if my father is on a mission. You can always tell when he has something important to say."

Paul twists his body towards the older man and is about to stand when he is interrupted.

"Don't bother." He then turns towards Anne. "Could you leave Paul and me alone for a short time." It really isn't a request, but rather an order.

Anne understands as she leaves. "Come get me when you're ready for my first lesson." She smiles brightly toward Paul who reciprocates with pleasure.

Without a good-morning or how-was-your-sleep introduction, Marcus gets to the point. "I have some disturbing news to tell you, and I do not want you to repeat it to anyone. Do you understand?" His voice is stern.

Surprised, Paul is at first silent. He is caught off guard. Then he shakes out of the daze. "Yes. You sound serious."

"More serious than you think. Someone tried to kill us, or perhaps only you."

Rendered speechless, Paul does not know what to say. Then he mutters, "Kill us, me?"

"That's what it looks like. The brakes in the Targa failed. They were tampered with. Deliberately." The words are spoken in an even pace, without much apparent emotion. Yet inside he is furious. He intends to find out who is responsible no matter how long it takes, and to make that person pay the ultimate price.

"How do you know?" Paul is still shocked by all of this. His voice is weak and quivering.

"My mechanic just inspected the car. He knows brakes."

"The car is old. Brakes fail."

"The brakes were messed with. He told me all about it. I believe him."

Talking aloud helps Paul shake off some of the disbelief, but not all. His throat feels dry and then suddenly he feels as if he is about to vomit. He coughs a few times. Then he manages to ask, "Why would anyone want to kill us? Kill me? What have I ever done to anyone? This is not possible. You've got it all wrong!" He shows signs of losing control of his emotions and thoughts, like a nearby bomb exploding, throwing off debris everywhere, and harming anyone and anything in close proximity.

"Settle down. You're alive."

Paul's eyes widen with the matter-of-fact comment. "Is that all you can say?"

"What else do you want me to say? Don't worry. Everything is going to be just fine."

"Yeah, something like that ... anything that isn't so ominous."

"Sorry."

Paul shakes his head, hoping to make sense out of it all. Nothing seems to come together right now, so he remains quiet. At least it gives him time to get control of his emotions. He senses his breathing is back on its natural rhythm. For some reason he smells a sweetness in the air that gets his brain working again. "Why did you really invite me here?" With the tables now turned on Marcus, Paul feels more self-confidence. The older man's face shows wrinkles that here-to-for were not apparent to him. He wonders why he hadn't noticed that before. He waits for a response from his host.

"To tutor my daughter. I thought the letter explained that nicely." The words sound flat.

"I don't believe you. Tell me the truth. Why did you bring me here?"

Marcus stands and turns his back to Paul. He wonders what he should say to the young man … how much truth he should reveal … how Paul might handle the truth. He does not have a high level of confidence that Paul can effectively deal with explosive information. Writers might script incidents of shock and scare that frighten their readers, but have they themselves even been involved in scary situations. He suspects not. He suspects Paul will not be able to deal with what he must say to him. Yet, he feels compelled to tell the truth. "I'm trying to find out who killed my son, Damien."

It is as if the wind is taken out of his sails, Paul feels sick to his stomach. He starts to gag but can't seem to heave the contents lodged deep inside. "Ugh." He doubles over.

Marcus turns to get a look at Paul's predicament. He lets the normal course of events take over, and within a few minutes the color of Paul's face returns to a more natural look. He walks closer to his guest and takes a seat nearby. "That's to be expected. I'd be quite surprised if you were unaffected." He pats the young man on the shoulders and gives him a sudden smile. "I've more to tell. Are you up to it?"

Paul manages to look up at the older man. A genuine look of anticipation appears on his face, yet he can't get the words out.

"Good. I need your help to find out who killed my son."

Paul's mouth opens wide, unable to get out a word for the moment. Then he takes a deep swallow to get his wits under control. "Kill! I thought he only disappeared?" As soon as the words leave his mouth he realizes he's made a big mistake.

Marcus gives him a stern look, stenciled with a definite expression of displeasure. The forbidding gloomy facial appearance sends a shiver up Paul's spine. "Disappeared? Who said anything about Damien disappearing? Tell me! Who's said this?" His nose and cheekbones fight for prominence in his face, settling for a draw.

It is Paul's turn to say something, anything that will get him out of this mess. His brain does not seem cooperative, but it must. He needs another chance to correct the error in judgment, or is it now too late? He begins to worry if things have already gotten out of hand.

"I said, who told you this? I demand you to tell me!"

Paul is not sure what the older man has actually said. The heat he feels build up inside is too consuming. It is as if his entire body is slowly boiling, simmering with heat that will eventually overtake him totally. He is not able to recognize sweat drip down his face, drops clinging to his chin.

Marcus steps forward and jabs Paul with a forefinger against his chest, hard enough for most people to feel some pain, but not sharp enough to inflict a wound.

The move shakes Paul out of his temporary daze, yet he is not sure what is going on. He blinks his eyes a few times as if that will reset his thoughts. It doesn't work fast enough.

Antonio Vianna

"There's only one person who would tell you." Marcus turns to walk away. Yet before he takes another step, a question is asked.

"Why do you think your son was killed?"

Marcus continues walking away, but then stops. "Because I know."

"Was there a body found?"

"Why are you asking me this? I know he was killed. I just know it."

"Maybe he ran away."

"Damien wouldn't do that, not my son … a little eccentric perhaps. He was a young boy then, but no, he wouldn't run away."

The words sound convincing enough to Paul, but there is a gap of doubt that still lingers with Marcus.

"Are you a cop?" Paul's voice is marked by an impassive matter of fact manner.

The question seems to be a strange one coming from the younger man. Marcus stops. He wrinkles his brow in slight confusion. "Why do you ask?"

Still in a deadpan manner, Paul says, "You don't talk like a cop, and you don't think like a cop. And certainly you don't act like a cop."

"So why do you ask me if I am a cop?"

"Because I know you're not an architect for sure, and now I'm trying to figure out who you really are, why you really brought me here.

Marcus tries to shift the burden of the conversation to a safer place. "How is a cop supposed to talk, think, and act?"

"Like an investigator, asking questions, digging and digging for real information, evidence, not just suppositions. You're not doing any of this, yet you say you know for certain Damien was killed."

Marcus pauses. "Are you a cop?"

It is Paul's turn to frown. "No. Why do you ask?" His voice now has an inquisitive sound to it.

Now fully facing Paul, Marcus looks him directly in the eyes. "Are you an investigator?"

"No, not really. I'm neither a cop nor an investigator."

Marcus hesitates for a split second. "I'll tell you why I brought you here." He stares at Paul. "I want you to act like a cop and an investigator."

"Huh?" A creepy feeling invades his psyche.

"You're a writer. Correct?"

"Yes, but what …."

"Writers do research, right?"

"I'm not following you. Where is this all headed?" Paul pauses just enough time to put some of the pieces together. "Oh, I see where you're going with this. So you think I can help you investigate your son's death through research methods."

"Partially."

"What's the full truth?"

"My son was killed, so let's get that straight. Don't listen to anyone who tells you differently. Second, I'm not the one who will investigate. You are the one who will investigate."

All of this is really another camouflage for putting Paul in the middle. Marcus has far more devious intentions. Yet, he will run into obstacles along the way as others raise the stakes to make their plans priority one.

"I'm not sure I want any part of this."

"You don't have a choice." The words are resolute and said unwaveringly.

"There's always a choice."

"Not this time."

Paul's line of questioning seems to have found a dead end. He is silent for a few seconds, not sure what next to say, if anything at all. He thought he was making some inroad, but now realizes that not to be the case. "Who knows about this?"

"About what?"

"Why I'm here. Your wife or daughter … do they know?"

"No."

"Why haven't you told them?"

"That will become clear to you when you begin your investigation."

"Do they believe your son was killed? Maybe he's just missing … or just ran away … or something else. Why do you think he was killed?"

"Again, you'll understand that better once you start."

Paul twists his face in a way that suggests he does not want to play the investigator role. He tries again to get out of it. "I'm not sure I'm your guy. I mean, I've never done this before, and to be perfectly honest, I think it's dangerous. I don't want any part of it."

"That's unfortunate."

"So you understand my quandary?"

"Oh, yes. I certainly understand your difficulty … I certainly do."

Paul gives him another quizzical look. "But there's more."

"Yes there is."

"Don't keep me in suspense. What is it?"

Marcus gives him a sneer. "I really don't give a rat's ass about your jam. You are here and you'll do what I ask you to do."

"You can't keep me here against my will. I can leave anytime I want. This is a free country." Paul's voice is tense and full of anxiety. He knows he is not nearly as convincing as he needs to be.

"Don't test me. I don't like being tested." A threatening grin returns.

The color of Paul's face begins to lose its natural condition. A sickly feeling returns.

"Take a sip of tea. There is more you need to learn about this house, my family, and my son's death. Remember, you have already been a target of death. I'm the only one here who is on your side. Regardless of whether you want to go through with your part, I'm the only one you can trust."

Paul unconsciously picks up the glass of tea and takes a long swallow, all the while eyeing Marcus, trying to figure a way out of the mess.

Elsewhere in the house, Elizabeth and Anne talk.

Antonio Vianna

"Father is talking with Paul."

"What about?"

"I'm not positive, but I suspect we both know."

"Damien?"

"Yes, that's my guess."

"Your father thinks he is so clever, bringing the young man here on the pretense of tutoring you. Sometimes I wonder if he thinks we are stupid."

"He is rather transparent at times, isn't he?"

"At times?"

"Well, mother, let's not be too harsh on him."

Elizabeth gives her daughter a grin that is a mixture of sympathy and bewilderment intended to be inadequate and insincere. They both think they know Marcus's underlying motives, but soon will discover they are only partially correct. He has more devious intentions.

"How do you intend to play along with Paul when he begins to tutor you? He'll find out rather quickly your intellect and broad interests."

"I think he's rather infatuated with me." She smiles coquettishly, knowing the power she has over most men. "I don't think that will be a problem."

Elizabeth understands. She too, as a younger woman, gained the attention and admiration of men without any sincere

56

affection towards them in return. Even today, she indulges on occasion with a playful flirt to get what she wants. The attitude seems to have been handed down to her daughter.

"Just don't take any unnecessary chances. Remember, if your father has his way with Paul, there will be two of them against the two of us. I think Paul can be easily manipulated. He seems somewhat naïve."

"And his simplicity could be to our advantage."

"Yes, it could, but it also could be to his benefit."

Anne wonders what her mother means. Before she can ask the question, Elizabeth explains.

"A simple mind asks all sorts of questions regardless of their relevance or importance, just as a child asks why over and over again. I'm not suggesting Paul is a child. Oh no. I'm only saying that he might ask so many questions that eventually he finds out what we have kept hidden. And ... we could not let that happen." Her once conversational-like smile turns serious.

Her mother's grave look is reflected in Anne's face. She clearly understands the message. She hesitates before asking, "So why don't we take the offense?"

"Excuse me? I'm not sure I understand." Elizabeth leans forward sensing her daughter has an important point to make that is worth hearing.

"I'm saying that maybe we should take the offense. You know, to prevent them from doing whatever it is they are intending to do."

Elizabeth smiles, expressing approval of the idea.

Recognizing her mother's acceptance of the notion she says, "So you like my suggestion?"

"Like mother like daughter." She shifts her body in the chair. "I've already started." She compliments herself with a big grin.

"Oh, mother! That's wonderful! What did you do?"

Before Elizabeth can answer, Anne adds, "Oh, wait a minute. I think I know."

"Tell me, dear. What?"

"Paul told me about hearing some noise in his room." She sees her mother's liking displayed on her face. "Then he told me he stepped out into the hallway where he believed the noise was coming from." Elizabeth's face glows. "He walked towards a door nearby that unexpectedly opened and closed." The two women continue looking at each other. "Mother, did you do that?"

Elizabeth bows her head as if she is humbly accepting an award. No words are needed.

"Bravo!" Anne exclaims as she claps her hands together. "Bravo!"

Elizabeth waves her right hand slightly as if to push aside the action as inconsequential. Yet, both women know the importance of putting doubt and fear into the mind of Paul.

"But we must do more." Anne says. She is now serious about furthering the plan.

"Here's what I'm thinking."

Chapter 3

While the Islands of Sanibel and Captiva are mostly hospitable to the locals and tourists, there are threats lurking everywhere. Pathways, trails, waterways and beaches all have hidden dangers. The lush surrounding can be a decoy to an otherwise safe place.

As with the bottle-nosed dolphin that frolics in the water, whose eyesight is excellent, these social animals must be aware of predators everywhere, just as with the human population. Both animal groups must constantly be on the look out to be safe. Chances are individuals within both animal species will not survive a normal life span. 'Safety First and Have Fun' is a common slogan one spots along the roadsides, yet many do not follow this simple reminder.

Across a small canal, within mangrove forests, live colorful birds of many types: blue herons, red egrets, and brown pelicans. Here they feed, rest, and preen. Amidst this serene like atmosphere are alligators that should be kept a safe distance away.

Antonio Vianna

Despite the fact that there are endless pleasures of nature, not everyone shares that same interest. Just like the birds that migrate to this coastal barrier island for temporary residence, some people come with harmful intentions.

Hidden away, amidst the island waters, rests a worn down barge, mostly sunk into the thick mud appearing smaller than its much larger size. Rusted in many places, it still is able to house one person, albeit in plain and simple living conditions. The original name on the stern has been chipped away over the years. It looks unsightly. Adjacent and hitched to the barge with a rope is a wooden oar boat, about six feet long. It too has an unpleasant appearance. The low hanging plant life helps in the camouflage.

The nineteen year old male inside the barge is not a happy camper. He's been in and out of juvenile confinement for the past several years since he ran away from his home. Given an early release from imprisonment and with little skill and knowledge base to find a legal and constructive job, he survives by scheming his way through life. He gets angrier and angrier. He has few ideas left in his limited brain bank, so after he takes a final swig of beer he heaves the empty can into a corner of the small room. It settles alongside its other companions accumulated over the months. He looks around for another six-pack but comes up empty handed.

Small pinholes of light sneak through the walls. It is humid inside the barge and reeks of stench. The man's bald head is clustered with insect bites that have failed to heal properly, mostly due to him scratching the affected areas. His otherwise pale white body is underweight showing signs of an unhealthy diet. He is dressed in military baggy shorts with no shirt. His chest is void of hair but displays a tattoo of two large swords crossing each other. He wears black sneakers.

Inhaling the stinking air is cumbersome for him, due to early signs of emphysema. He spits up phlegm that temporarily helps out. The young man struggles to stand, his head buzzing from consuming alcohol, as he looks around for something. Coming up empty handed he walks a few feet towards a cardboard box that contains several tee-shirts with a variety of slogans and symbols on their front and back. He picks one at random and stares at its message for a few seconds, *Grab for the Gusto*. He pulls it over his head. Wobbling just a little, he flops his body on the metal floor to wait until dark before he leaves the barge to oar his way to the nearest place to steal more beer.

He dozes off for a while until night settles in. A few hours later he wakes up. Then he stuffs into his shorts an old .45 automatic and makes his way towards a ten foot metal ladder to climb topside where the air is cooler and fresher. Once outside he takes in a deep breath.

The small wooden boat is exactly where he left it. He compliments himself for small achievements. He gets into the boat and begins to oar, weaving his way through the thickets, guided by the moon's light. He reaches a place where he safety hides the boat for a short time until he finishes the rest of his task. Soon he is within eyesight of a store.

The man touches the revolver in his shorts for comfort and looks around to spot one vehicle parked outside the building.

Antonio Vianna

He wonders if he should wait until the place has no customers, or if that really matters. He decides to take action now.

He bolts into the store, "This is a stick up. Don't anybody move." The words are a bit slurred from the effects of alcohol and the tone is high strung.

Two men are facing each other at a counter just ahead. The night time clerk is about to give the customer change. For a brief second they freeze.

"Don't move. I got a gun." His hand shakes a bit as he wipes his nose with the back of his free hand.

Paul is about to turn around but is quietly cautioned by the cashier to remain still. He obeys the advice.

The man moves quickly. Soon he is side by side the other two men. "Give me your cash." He turns the revolver towards the cashier.

"Don't shoot. Here … take the money." His voice quivers and is high pitched.

Paul waits in silence.

"You, give me your wallet."

Paul feels the coldness of the gun's metal nozzle against his back. He eyes his billfold on the counter top.

"Give it to me!" The man is now impatient with what he believes to be defiance.

"It's on the counter … right there … see!" His voice is full of fear.

The young man reaches for the wallet as the cashier presses a red button below the counter to summons the police. The move goes unnoticed by the two other men.

Satisfied he's gotten more than what the original plan called for, he steps back. On his way out, he grabs a six pack of beer. He runs for safety.

Now racing as fast as his legs will take him, he hears sirens from an approaching police car. He seems to be galloping, giving preference to his left side, heart starting to race to keep up with the pace.

A policeman spots him as the young man edges towards a cluster of bushes. The police vehicle screeches to a stop. The officer begins his chase on foot covering the same ground more easily, but the young man knows exactly where to head to get away.

Now out of sight and clouds obscuring the moon's light, the policeman is not able to continue the pursuit. He saw the young man run down a particular path, yet somehow he disappeared. The officer waits in silence, hoping to pick up some sound in the thicket, something to lead him in the robber's direction.

The dense foliage and thick branches give the young man his only protection. He remains put until he feels it is safe to oar back to the barge. The delay is a short time, and soon he is guzzling down a can of beer. He lets out a fart.

Now joined by the police officer, the store cashier and Paul explain the robbery as best they can, including the description of the young man. Their stories are remarkably similar to the officer's satisfaction.

"He's got my wallet … with all my identification. He could rip me off." Paul is still quivering from the experience.

"My best advice is to contact your credit card issuers as soon as possible," the police officer says in a matter of fact manner, too accustomed to the situation to show much more compassion and sympathy.

"Sure." As if talking aloud to himself, Paul continues, "I've got to get a new driver's license, new library card, …" He pauses, "Oh, hell, I think my social security number is compromised! Damn it!"

The store cashier does not seem to care much about his customer's personal problems. "I'm not looking forward to telling my boss about this. He's going to be real pissed. I just know it."

Ignoring both men's troubles, the police officer says, "Here is my card. If you think of anything else that might help us apprehend the robber, let me know. We may be calling on you in the future to testify if we find the guy."

"What are the chances of finding him … the real odds?" the cashier asks, knowing all along what the answer will be.

The police officer glances back and forth between the cashier and his note pad, "Not much."

"Figured." The cashier shakes his head sideways.

The police office ignores the comment. He closes his note pad and walks away.

Paul and the cashier are left alone with not much to say to each other.

Stranger on a Train

Now settled down a little, the young man grabs a second beer. He takes only a sip before he picks up the wallet. Surprised to find over two hundred dollars in cash, he lets out a loud roar. He tosses aside the credit cards, knowing he'd have a tough time using them. Yet, two other documents attract his attention.

The driver's license is from California, and there is a white piece of paper with a local Sanibel address. He almost drops the beer can when he recognizes the location. Thoughts collide with one another preventing him to make sense of anything. He takes another gulp from the beer can, this time a long one. His breathing picks up a little too fast to his liking, so he takes in a deep breath of air to calm down. He lets out a cough from the disgusting smell.

Since he knows the area well he begins thinking about what to do next. He leans back with closed eyes to concentrate but soon is asleep.

Later that same evening, Paul returns to his temporary residence to find Marcus alone reading *Hidden Dangers*, a

Antonio Vianna

novel. He looks up as Paul walks towards him. "You seem a little weary."

Paul moves closer and takes a seat, letting out a sigh of exhaustion. "I was robbed." His voice lacks the usual excitement.

Marcus rests the book on his chest, now looking somewhat puzzled. "Robbed? Are you alright?"

Looking straight ahead at no one in particular, Paul says, "I was driving around a little trying to figure some things out from this afternoon's conversation. I stopped off at the beach to clear my head, and then before I realized it, it was getting dark. I hadn't eaten since lunch so I decided to stop off at a place to get a sandwich and something to drink. The only place I could find was a convenience-like store."

Marcus isn't sure where the story is headed so he decides to keep quiet. He figures Paul is talking through something of importance.

"Then, all of a sudden as I was paying for my food, this guy barges in. He takes my wallet and the money from the cash register. It happened so fast. I've never been robbed before."

Marcus stays silent knowing there is more to come.

"The cashier must have secretly contacted the police because as the guy was running away a cop showed up … he got away."

Marcus has now placed the book on a nearby table and his arms are folded over his chest. He looks intently at Paul, worried that the young man's nerves are frail, and selfishly wonders if he can still play a central role in his plans. He begins to second guess his original reasoning to involve him.

66

"I've got to notify the issuers of my credit cards, get another driver's license, … ugh … this is not good … no this is not good at all."

He feels now is the time to intervene. "Paul, I know you've been through an ordeal, but you are alive. You were not harmed. The only real things you need to worry about are administrative, nothing more. I can help you get through this. Don't worry. It'll soon be over with. Trust me on this, I know."

They say timing is everything, and perhaps it is timing in this case as well or might it be something else. Paul begins to feel a little more relieved now that Marcus has spoken. Is it the sound of Marcus's voice, like an old priest telling him everything will work out as long as he has faith? He feels he can trust the man sitting in front of him … the man who brought him here to tutor his daughter, but who has other plans for him. Paul sneaks out a smile that seems to be calming to him. He takes in a deep breath yet all the while there is an itch he can't seem to scratch, wondering if he is strong enough to carry on.

"How about a nightcap before we turn in." Marcus stands and heads for a cabinet where he pulls out two stemmed glasses and a bottle of Amaretto di Saronno. Then he adds, "I want Anne's lessons to begin tomorrow once you complete those administrative chores."

The itch returns.

Antonio Vianna

By noon the next day Paul finishes off the last of his phone calls, temporarily relieved the chore is out of the way. His attention now turns to Anne, whose first lesson is about to begin later on in the afternoon. He figures tutoring Anne will be the most pleasurable thing he's been able to do thus far. A smile appears on his face anticipating the meeting.

He begins arranging a few books he intends to discuss with her. He decides to use a wide variety of authors and genres at first, and then narrow down the selection once they've met a few times. Consumed in the planning process, he soon is fully absorbed and overlooks the passing of time. He hears a knock on his bedroom door. He looks up.

"Paul, are you in there?"

He recognizes Anne's voice.

"I thought we were going to meet at two. It's now half past the hour. Am I mistaken about the time of our first lesson?"

He glances at his wristwatch to realize he's missed the first appointment. "Oh my gosh, I've lost track of time. I'll be down in five minutes."

"I'll be waiting for you."

He jumps to his feet and gathers a few books, notepaper, and a pen. Soon he joins Anne in a downstairs drawing room.

"I thought you'd perhaps forgotten. I was getting a little worried that my personal tutor was bailing out on me." She smiles brightly his way.

He enjoys her tease. Hoping there is more to come he tries a little himself. "I wouldn't do that to you without giving you proper notice." He waits to see if she picks up.

"And what would a proper notice be?" She gives him a little pout that is mixed in with a seductive grin.

"A formal letter, of course, that was grammatically written and properly addressed."

Now run out of wordplay, he hopes she too is ready to end the banter, but he is wrong.

"Formality is, oh, all so formal." She frowns as if she is pondering something of importance. "There doesn't seem to be any flexibility to do whatever you really feel like doing." She moves a little closer to him, now eyes wider than before, and focused directly on his lips. "Sometimes, I just like to let it happen naturally … know what I mean?" She laughs just a little but there isn't a bit of humor in it.

He understands where the conversation is headed, and while he would like to take it to the next level, he decides now is not the time or the place. It isn't their age differences so much as it is other things. He figures maybe six or seven years separate them which isn't much. It's his responsibility to her father, the man who hired him to tutor her, and just recently he found out, to help investigate his son's circumstances. In a way he scorns himself for being so responsible. Maybe he needs to follow Anne's advice, to do what he feels like doing. However, he concludes now is not the time to make that change.

"Yes, I know what you mean." He gives her a polite smile that tells it all.

She pulls back yet self-assured there will be a more suitable time in the near future. Remember, she's told him she is psychic.

"I've brought a few books that we should start discussing. Perhaps you've already read them. If so, then we can get right into it. If not, then I'll give you a little summary of the author and something about the book before I assign you what I think you need to read. Essentially I want to determine your level of understanding, breadth and depth, of some of the more important authors and their works before we get into the real nitty-gritty. Ok?"

"Sounds like a plan." Her response is more akin to a student answering a question from the teacher. She knows how to play her role.

"Let's start with a novel by George Eliot, *The Mill on the Floss*. Have you read it?"

"In their death, they were not divided." She gives him a scholarly grin, displaying her knowledge.

"I guess you have." He responds with an approving nod, and then moves on to another selection.

Two hours later Anne says, "I'm exhausted. Can we call it quits?"

Paul looks at her realizing his level of literary enthusiasm is not fully shared by his pupil. While he believes her to be well-read and seemingly cultured in many ways, he makes a mental note to keep in check his passion for reading and writing.

"Of course. Sometimes, I get too involved in matters that others don't find as interesting." He waits for her to say something. When she remains silent, he continues. "Take this." He hands her a copy of C. S. Lewis's *Out of the Silent Planet*, which is the first volume of his Space Trilogy. "Have you read it?" He hopes she has not.

"No, I'm not into that stuff."

"Good that you haven't read his works, and no problem about not enjoying fantasy and science fiction. *Out of the Silent Planet* is as good as it gets. I compare it to Camus's *The Plague* for its moral issues. Have you read anything by Camus?"

She shrugs her shoulders, not sure, which he takes as a green light to go on.

"Oh. Anyway, as you read this, consider the moral implications that arise from the book's main character, Dr. Elwin Ransom. Then we'll discuss it together."

She looks at him, quizzically, prepared to ask a question. He gets there before she does.

"That's right. I'll be asking you to read a number of books, hopefully those you haven't yet read. Then, we'll talk."

"Can you be more specific? Talk about what?"

"For starters, thematic elements, such as the plot, the mood, the characters, the structure, the ideas."

"Hmm, nothing about the writing style?"

"Oh, for certain. We'll discuss writing style and what makes a good story."

"Ok, what makes a good story?"

"A good story is unified in its plot, is credible, is interesting, is both simple and complex, and generates emotion from the reader. There's more, of course, but we'll get into that later on. First, I want you to read the books I give you, starting with this one, focusing in on the moral issues. Then we'll get into the other aspects of writing."

"Are you going to ask me to write something?" She seems a little hesitant with the question.

He smiles, "Of course. The only way a writer improves is by writing."

"Oh." She seems slightly troubled.

"Don't be worried. I'm not going to show it to anyone. It's just between you and me." He gives her a genuine smile realizing the uneasiness that often accompanies new writers.

She doesn't like the idea of putting her ideas on paper. People can interpret the words anyway they want, to serve their own purpose. She searches for a way to mitigate her mental agitation, as some people do with worry beads when they roll the string of beads between their fingers to preoccupy their concerns.

He senses her growing anxiety, not sure what to make of it. "But that won't be for quite a while. You'll feel better by then." His smile is now forced and he senses she picks up on it.

She clears her throat, pushing away the writing part of the lesson. "When do we meet again? I can't possibly finish this book in a day."

"When can you finish it?"

"Oh, I suppose in three days. Yes, I will finish it three days from today." She seems hopeful about the commitment.

"Then, we shall get together then to talk about the book."
He pauses. Is there more to come? He stares at her, admiring
her beauty, flashing back to his rebuke of her previous sexual
tease. He keeps quiet.

Anne wonders if the lesson has ended. "Are we done for
the day, or do you have additional assignments for me?" She
is not sure.

He shakes out of the trance-like state. "No ... I mean
yes ... we are done for today." He shifts his body in the chair
suddenly feeling awkward.

In another part of the house, Marcus and Elizabeth are in
an intense conversation.

"Don't lie to me, Elizabeth! You're not very good are
lying."

"Don't you ever accuse me of lying, or I'll ..."

"You'll what ... cut me off from my allowance?"

"At least you remember who's paying the bills around
here!" Her eyes are black with fury.

The reminder seems to settle him down, but only for a few
seconds. He has not been scratched from the horse race just
yet. "It's no sense trying to carry on a normal conversation with
you. You just won't listen."

"Me?" The wrath intensifies. "You won't get it out of your
thick head that Damien was not killed. He left this house
because he was fed up with it all ... especially you."

Antonio Vianna

"So now I am to blame for everything ... is that it ... is that how it works?"

"Marcus, you were never around when he was growing up ... off traveling around the world ... acting as if you were a real architectural consultant."

"I studied two years in Italy. I have a certificate to prove it."

"We both know how much that certificate ... if you can call it as such ... really cost me. It was purchased, Marcus. Have you forgotten?"

"I studied for two years." The redundancy falls on deaf ears.

"As you wish ... as you dream." A tone of repugnancy fills the air as silence cuts between them. She continues. "When you returned from your studies, as you say, you turned your back on your only son, our son. There wasn't anything he could do to please you. You were constantly on his back, criticizing everything he did."

"He was a strange child."

"But he was your child," she reminds him. "Our child."

"He wouldn't listen to anything I told him."

"That was the main problem."

He gives her a questioning look, not sure what she means.

"You told him ... not asked him. It was always giving orders without listening to what he might have to say about it all."

"He was just a child! Was I supposed to listen to a child?"

"Yes … I did." Her voice is resolute and calm.

Silence claims center stage again.

Then she jumps back into taking the lead. "He left this family … God knows where he may have gone … even if he is still alive. I wonder about him. So does Anne. She misses her brother deeply." The tone is subdued, almost as if she is whispering something to a friend in church.

"He was killed." Marcus seems to ignore the comment, and like a terrier dog that won't let go of a pants leg, hangs onto the opinion.

She shakes her head, exasperated by his bullheadedness.

"I can only image what you've told Paul since he arrived." The statement is intended to be a question, but it does not come out that way. She waits for a response that is slow in coming.

"I wrote him …"

"I know what you wrote him. That wasn't my question." Her anger seeps into the response.

"I hadn't realized you asked me a question." His cleverness does not work this time.

"Don't get smart with me! What have you told him since he arrived?" Her voice is now heightened.

He's been through her tirades before, so he is not shocked at all. He figures she will settle down after a while, so he keeps quiet a little longer. The tactic does not work as he had hoped.

"Are you now deaf? I've asked you a simple question." The ranting continues.

Antonio Vianna

He thinks about walking away, to get out of the situation, but knows that would only be a short term solution. He decides to stay engaged with her as best he knows how, reminding himself that she controls the finances, and he could not carry on his life style without her money. He bites his lip, deciding to lie his way out, a mistake he has not learned to correct.

"Nothing."

"Nothing? You can't think I believe that!"

"It's the truth … so help me." He is without much expression.

Elizabeth doubts he is being honest, but lets it go for the time being. He'll be judged soon enough. She decides to alter the topic. "Has Paul and Anne met for their first lesson?" Her voice is more conciliatory now.

The change in subject and sound of her voice takes him by surprise. He is not sure how to respond, so he waits a few seconds. "I think they were to meet this afternoon to develop some sort of lesson plan, or something." He gives himself a silent compliment believing it to be a reasonable assertion.

She flickers her eyebrows as if to confirm his statement, something that pleases him greatly. He passes to himself another secret compliment.

Hoping this has finally ended their talk, he starts to move away. She stops him with another question.

"Who do you really think tampered with the Porsche's brakes?"

His eyes widen from surprise. "I'm not sure, but I mean to find out." Then without much further consideration he blurts,

"Elizabeth, to be perfectly honest with you, I did ask Paul to do something after he arrived here."

"And what was that?"

"I asked him to help me investigate what or who may have caused the brakes to fail. I should have told you this earlier, but, well, I figured not to concern you or Anne. I suspect he and I will be gone a few hours together here and there, away from the house. That's what we'll be doing … looking into the brakes' failure."

She wonders if this is a half truth, of if there is more to it. She has her own plan regardless of whatever he has up his sleeve. "Thank you for telling me."

Each realizes the other is up to something, but specifically what that might be remains a mystery to each of them for now. They sit quietly, looking at each other. The silence is overwhelming.

"Am I interrupting something?"

Anne's voice breaks the standoff as their bodies jump ever so slightly with the unexpected arrival of their daughter.

She suspects something is up with her parents, another argument she guesses. She's broken in before without announcing herself to catch them going at it. Her voice now is low and whispering, almost as if she is holding back. "Maybe I'll come back another time." She starts to turn away.

"No, dear, come join us. We were just finishing up." Her mother forces one of those insincere but well intended motherly smiles to calm things over.

Anne goes on. "I can come back later. Really I can."

Marcus's glare could bore through a steel plate. His eyes say it all, yet he remains quiet.

Everyone knows another heated argument has just taken place. They all know it to be true, but not willing to admit it openly in front of each other, especially with Anne's presence.

She gets up enough courage. "I know you've been at it again, tossing grenades back and forth. I'm not a child anymore." While her voice may sound firm, she wonders if she is the only one to hear her keep in check sobbing breaths. She wishes they would end the constant squabbling. At times it seems to be a power struggle between her parents over something she is not sure of, although something she suspects. She promises not to let this happen to her marriage, if that should ever happen.

"Come here dear. Sit by us. You are one calming force in our family. Please, come." Elizabeth motions with her hand while Marcus continues to fume.

Anne moves forward to take her place by her mother. She says to herself in silence, "I can't do this many more times."

Now standing Marcus says, "Have you met with Paul yet?" He hopes the change of topic calms things down.

Delighted with the amended mood Anne says, "Yes. He certainly is very knowledgeable about books. I'm hoping to learn much from him." Her eyes match the pleasant sound of her voice.

"He should be. He's a writer." He clamps his lips together, admonishing the sarcasm.

Elizabeth shakes her head in disbelief, and then moves on to something more positive. "Yes, I suspect Paul has a wide assortment of books to discuss with you. I'm very happy you are pleased. You'll have to tell us more along the way."

"Oh yes, mother. I will."

Still standing Marcus says, "Yes, yes." His voice is limp, like a plate of overcooked linguine. "You'll have to fill us in." He seems totally bored.

No one seems to be ready to carry on with conversation at the moment, each in their separate thoughts.

Feeling out of place as if he had just interrupted a private conversation, Marcus says, "I've got a few things to do." He walks away a little hurried as people do when they have some place important to go, or when they are trying to get away as fast as possible. In this case, it might be the latter.

Hiding behind a curtain Paul remains still. While the weather conditions outdoors seem to be tranquil, a storm is brewing inside the house. For a split second he considers leaving this place to get back home, to be where it is safer and without all this commotion. Yet, he stays put. Is it curiosity that takes control of him, or is it something else?

Whispers inside the nearby room coach him to inch closer. He steps nearer to the hushed sounds. Clumsily he knocks against a table. It slides an inch or less against the marble floor making a sound he hopes only reaches his ears. He steadies both the table and himself, anticipating a reaction from the two women. The seconds tick away as if becoming hours. He presses his luck and advances another step, yet this time looking at the floor to make sure nothing is in his way. Unfortunately, the move is not sufficient to conceal his presence. He looks up to see Elizabeth and Anne staring at him. His face turns reddish.

"Were you eavesdropping, Paul?" Elizabeth's question is apparent as seemingly is the answer.

Should he contrive a story or tell the truth? "I … I was simply passing by." He swallows but his mouth is dry. "To be honest, the conversation was rather loud that it was impossible not to overhear parts of it." He looks away for a split second before continuing. "I had no intention of purposely listening in … but … well…" He shrugs his shoulders not sure what else to say. The less the better he figures.

It is Anne's turn to say something. "We were shouting, mother." She appears to sympathize with him or does she have another goal in mind?

"Yes, I suppose we all were a little excited and might have talked too loudly." The words do not match the sincerity of her voice, yet she lets it pass. "Is there something you were looking for as you passed by?"

Surprised to be let off the hook without much grilling he accepts the gesture as a gift and leaves it alone. "Umm, no. Just walking around. Nothing more to it than that." He knows they suspect something else.

"So it is." Elizabeth pauses, and then goes on. "Would you like to join us and have something to drink? It might be the precise tonic we need now."

"Yes, Paul. Please join us." Anne's voice is full of energy and refreshing to his ears.

He feels stimulated. "Thank you. That sounds like a great idea."

"Anne, why don't you mix up your award winning Pimm's Cup for the three of us."

"Have you had one before?" Anne asks Paul.

"I don't think so, but I'm willing to try."

Anne leaves Elizabeth and Paul alone, initially in silence until one of them figures out how to start a conversation. She solves the problem first. "So, Paul, how has your stay with us been thus far?"

It seems like an innocuous question, but he wonders if there is more to it. He decides to play it safe. "Well, I'm pleased that Anne and I have had our first lesson. She seems eager to learn."

She offers him a polite smile that is neither sincere nor fake, just an automatic facial response. "That's nice to hear. I'm not surprised. She is an eager beaver in many ways."

He flashes back to Anne's sexual tease and agrees on her mother's assessment. "I hope I can live up to her expectations."

"To be honest, few people are able to keep pace with her. You've got your hands full."

He wonders if she is warning him of something to come, or if the comment is innocuous. He shrugs it off as soon as Anne appears carrying a tray with three tall beverage glasses of drink.

Antonio Vianna

She offers one first to her mother, and then to Paul. Finally, she sets the tray on a table and proposes a toast. "To our happiness, forever and ever."

Sitting alone inside the barge, the young man thinks about his next move. He reaches for another beer, pops it open and takes a long swallow. He wonders why the customer whose wallet he took has this particular address written on a piece of paper. Is he a friend just visiting or is he on business? He gulps another ounce or so of beer. Nothing comes to mind, so he continues to wonder.

He looks around for something to eat. Alcohol makes him hungry. So, he heads towards a tiny kitchen area where he keeps nonperishable food. There is a large opened bag of potato chips that look promising. He grabs the yellow colored bag and reaches inside for a handful. He stuffs his mouth with as much as he can. Pieces of uneaten chips rest on his lips that go unnoticed. He takes another sip of beer to quench his thirst. He likes the combination. He repeats the process until the entire bag is empty.

With hunger pains partially satisfied, he takes in a deep breath and figures to head off to find out more about Paul Autore. He is sure he remembers how to get to the house. It hasn't been that long since he left.

Stranger on a Train

Now outside in the night's warm humid air, he gets into the wooden oar boat. In a short time, the boat is hidden and he begins to make his way. Soon he is in sight of the building.

The house no longer looks foreboding to him as it once did. He wonders why that may be. Unable to come to any conclusion, he casts aside the thought. There are more important things to do right now. He moves slowly around, trying not to make any noise. The adrenalin pump that worked so well when he first started out is still functioning well. He has a hard time controlling his emotions.

The pale moon light casts its appearance on the front door. The yard is empty and neat as he remembered it when he lived there with no sign that anyone might be inside. To the contrary, there are people sleeping within the house, yet in another way, strange as it may seem, he considers there really isn't anybody inside.

He wonders if the secret door is still accessible, the one he often used to go out at night and return when his parents and sister were asleep. There is only one way to determine that. He creeps a little faster now that he is closer to the building, still intending to be quiet. He feels his heart beat fast, something that turns him on. Now at the northeast side of the building he shoves aside a few bushes. A big smile comes over his face. The small door is directly in front of him. He looks more closely.

Now, there is a padlock securing the passageway. "No problem," he whispers to himself. He pulls out a fine tool in the shape of a thin piece of metal. He inserts its tip into the lock's miniature hole and then gives it a few twists back and forth until he hears a metallic click. His eyes light up. He removes the lock and sets it on the ground in view as a reminder to reinstall it when he leaves. He opens the small wooden door and looks in.

There are a few spider webs attached to the sides of the passageway so he wipes them off with his hand so that he can begin crawling his way to his former bedroom. While he is taller now than when he was younger, his overall thin size should not be an obstacle for him to easily work his way through the passageway. He has no planned idea what to do once he reaches the end of the crawlspace, but figures he'll think of something when that time comes. He begins his journey.

He feels a weird sensation come over himself as he moves within the tunnel-like space. It is as if he is traveling backward in time from one place to another, from adolescence to childhood. A shiver comes over his body. Recollections of past experiences flash through his mind. He lets the memories fade away as fast as they arrive.

While without a flashlight or something to illuminate his advance, he figures he's about half way to his destination. He rests a little. Crawling on his hands and knees is more tiresome than he anticipated. As a kid, he had unlimited energy. Now older and totally out of shape, he needs to properly allocate his energy. Five minutes pass and he moves on.

He remembers that up ahead is a steeper incline that will take him to the second floor. There are step like boards on the floor side of the tunnel that will help him climb. He hopes they are still in place and sturdy enough to hold his heavier body.

Stranger on a Train

No turning back now, so he advances, but now, more slowly. The rise is his adversary.

Finally, he feels a series of five small wooden slats nailed to the floor of the tunnel representing the end is near. He crawls slowly now, extending his hands, alternatively ahead, to touch the small door that hides this end of the tunnel. Suddenly, he feels what he's been waiting for. He gives himself a broad grin. "Yeah" he murmurs to himself.

He takes another break before continuing. He is uncertain what next to do. He knows the door leads into a small clothes closet. He hopes there is no obstruction on the other side. But what next? What does he want to do? He still isn't sure, so he remains put for a little while longer.

Suddenly, he hears a noise, not sure what to make of it. He listens. The toilet flushes. He realizes there is someone in his former bedroom who just took a pee. Now's not the time to test whether the small door will open. He can't turn around in the tunnel, so his only choices are to wait a while longer until the person falls asleep, or else to crawl backwards until he reaches the other side. Neither option seems optimal to him. So, he stretches his thin gawky-like body to wait for a decision.

An answer comes sooner than he expected. He hears a squeaky sound from the door hinges that need oiling. He is not sure what to make of it all so he waits it out. More sound comes from someone carefully stepping on the old wooden floor, and then the sound of a female voice.

"Paul, are you awake?" The voice is soft and sweet. Coils from the bed spring react to the weight of a second person's body.

"Huh?" The male voice sounds surprised. He sits up in the bed.

"It's me. I've come to comfort you." The alluring sound is irresistible. She tries to snuggle close to him but he shoves his body away.

"What are you doing here?"

"What do you think? I'm not here to recite a page from one of your books. Just relax."

The alleged proposition is awfully tempting to him. He feels himself getting aroused. "No, this is not right." He pushes her away. After the words leave his mouth he wants to change them, but can't. It's too late, or is it. Why can't he reconsider?

She persists. "Didn't mother tell you I usually get what I want? I'm sure she did. And you know what I want now, don't you."

"Yes, but not now. No, not now."

"Aren't I attractive to you?"

"It's not that. It's …."

"Are you attracted to men, is that it?"

"Of course not. No. I like women."

"Then what's your problem?"

"Honestly? I don't think your parents would approve."

"So, should I ask them? Would that solve your problem?"

Stranger on a Train

"Be serious."

"I am very serious."

"Yes, I know, and that might be the problem."

"I don't get it. You're my tutor, tell me."

"Oh, no, don't twist my job here with you."

"So, all I am is a job. Nothing else?"

"Anne, just leave. There is no sense of talking about this further."

"Now you sound just like my father, ordering me what to do." She puts her hands to her face and lets out a whimper of a cry.

He is not sure if she is faking it or if it is real, but he feels the urge to comfort her. He takes hold of her, bringing her body close to his. She feels warm. He feels hot. She lifts her face just enough to give him a deep kiss that sends endless tingles from his toes to his head. He does not resist, wrapping his arms around her tightly. She pushes him backwards onto the bed, resting her body atop his, moving her pelvis against him. He feels he is out of control. Suddenly, just when she is ready to ride him, he turns away. She flops aside, surprised by his unexpected move. She is speechless.

He is now breathing heavily, yet trying to simmer down. He can't believe what he's just done, wanting to erase the last frame. However, it is too late.

"You are quite the charmer," she says sarcastically as she shakes her head in disbelief. "I think the problem is that you've never done it before." She gets out of bed and walks towards the bedroom door. "I'm not through with you. I'll be the first and the best you've ever had. Trust me." She leaves him alone in bed.

"Unbelievable," he says to himself in a low voice. The gawky man in the secret tunnel shakes his head. He is tempted to make himself known to Paul, to give him the low down on the family, each and every one, but decides that not to be a good idea, at least not now. He waits a little longer for Paul to fall asleep.

During the next several minutes he hears bed spring coils move up and down telling the story of a restless man. He rests his head sideways, right ear to the floor of the tunnel, to take a break himself. Breathing is now a little easier, so he closes his eyes.

He quickly dozes off for a short time and then awakes, not sure how long he's been asleep. There really is no way since he is inside a dark passageway without a watch. Hearing no sound from the bedroom he decides to try to push open the small door just ahead. To his surprise it moves without much pressure. He squints to see the inside of his old closet smelling the same odor he remembered some time ago, yet, in a strange way, it seems as if it was only recently.

He shimmies his way out of the tunnel, finding himself flat on the closet floor. He hesitates before moving further, listening to anything that might be an alarm for him to quit. Satisfied it is safe to continue he stands straight, arcs his back to loosen up tightened muscles. He opens the closet door slightly to take a peep through. Thinking the bed has not been moved to another location in the room, he looks straight ahead to spot a man sprawled out on top of the covers. This must be Paul. Who else would it be?

As silent as he can be, he steps forward. The floor boards sound his presence, but there is nothing he can do about it. He gives the man a good look over, recognizing him from the driver's license photo he now holds in his hand. "Yep, it's you alright," his voice purposely muffled.

Standing only two feet from Paul, he turns towards a nearby stand. Lying on top of the piece of furniture is a magazine he recognizes. He picks up *Car Maintenance and Repair* as if it was a lost heirloom. He looks at it with a great deal of pleasure wondering if the man in front of him shares the same interests as he. Thinking for only a few fleeting seconds he decides to swap the magazine with something else. He replaces the publication with Paul's driver's license. "That's fair and square," he mumbles without much sound.

Paul suddenly makes an abrupt noise as he turns his body to the side. A fart lingers in the air.

Considering his visit to be completed, the young man returns to the closet and retraces his movements to find safety out doors. "I'll be back," he says as he relocks the door. With *Car Maintenance and Repair* in hand, Damien disappears into the dark.

Chapter 4

Marcus restlessly sits drinking a cup of coffee, fidgeting all the while as he waits for Paul. While no official meeting is scheduled between the two men, edginess still persists. He gulps down the last remains of the dark liquid with one swallow and then starts to get a refill. Halfway to the coffee pot, he stops for a second as if to consider something of importance. He checks his watch. It is close to 10:00 AM. He places the coffee cup on the countertop and heads upstairs. He hurries as if time is of the essence.

Now at the top of the stairs he eyes Paul's bedroom door and without any hesitation briskly walks towards it. Without knocking he opens the door to find the younger man still in bed. "Hey! Get up!"

The sound startles Paul as his body jumps. He turns over to see an agitated man looking straight down at him. He rubs his eyes as if to wipe away the image. It doesn't work.

"Time to get up! We have work to do." Marcus walks around the bed to find an empty chair adjacent to a furniture stand. He takes a seat not yet noticing the driver's license resting on top.

Still not sure what to make of it all, Paul follows the older man's moves in silence. Irritation begins to creep its way into his psyche. He's never liked being abruptly interrupted from sleep. He has no idea what is really happening.

"What are you waiting for? Do you want me to help you get up?" He's always loved pushing and shoving to get what he wants. This time is no exception.

"What are you doing here? Is the house on fire?"

"Your ass will burn after I kick it if you don't get up now. It's past ten in the morning." He taps his fingers on top of the furniture stand.

"You sure are a strange one, a great character for my next psycho drama."

The message does not make the impact Paul had hoped for, bouncing off Marcus as a basketball rebounding from hitting a hardwood floor. Should he try a second time, or should he try another approach?

He takes a deep breath and swings his legs across the bed. Now standing in his shorts he stretches just long enough to annoy Marcus. He gives himself a silent grin. "You'll excuse me. I need to take a pee, unless you want to watch." Another smirk to himself, but this time it seeps out just enough for Marcus to notice. Paul walks into the bathroom to take care of business.

Left alone in the bedroom, Marcus looks around, short bursts of remembrances rapidly flash by. Nothing has changed much in this room. While wetted to the belief that his son was killed, he has no tangible evidence. Could he be mistaken as his wife and daughter constantly remind him, as the authorities have told him, or is it all a conspiracy to keep something from him? He'd give almost anything to find out what really happened to his son. He is unyielding in his commitment to find out the truth, whatever it takes, whatever the pain may be. Small drops of water edge their way to the corners of his eyes. He quickly rubs them away. No time for needless sensitivities creeping in the way. There is too much work to do.

Paul exits the bathroom, finished taking care of business. Shaven and hair combed he heads for the closet to find clothes. He grabs a shirt off a hanger and then a pair of pants. Now ready to get into his socks and shoes he suddenly stops. There seems to be something different that he can't quite figure out. He continues to look at the floor for a few more seconds. What is it, he wonders to himself? What am I seeing that doesn't make sense? His inner thoughts are interrupted.

"We're not headed to a fashion show! Get a move on!"

Paul shrugs his shoulders, prepared to forget about it for now. He grabs the nearest pair of shoes and socks to finish dressing.

Now ready, both men are about to leave the bedroom when Marcus says, "Do you always leave your driver's license lying around like this? It's a good way to lose it." He glances between Paul and the plastic coated card.

Furrows take hold on his forehead, not sure he clearly heard Marcus's message.

"It's up to you. It's your driver's license."

Paul makes a quick move toward the furniture stand. He is surprised what he sees. "This … this was in my wallet when it was stolen! How did it get here?"

"Say again?" Now both men are startled.

Paul wonders if last night's visit by Anne has anything to do with this. Could she have placed it there? How could she have gotten hold of it since it was stolen by a man, a youngish, bald-headed, scrawny-looking man? What's the connection, if there is any? He is not able to make sense of any of it, and for certain, he is not about to tell Marcus that his daughter made a visit last night to sexually seduce him. He concludes a good old fashion lie is in order. "I'm mistaken. I guess it was here all along. Let's go. Tell me what we have to do today."

Marcus thinks nothing of Paul's situation, too interested in getting down to some business with the younger man. He shrugs his shoulders showing off his indifference. However, he should pay more attention to understanding how the driver's license ended up in the room. It would make it a whole lot easier for him.

Both men leave the bedroom together.

In a garage nearby Julien opens boxes that contain parts to repair the Porsche's brakes. Classical music plays in the background soft enough not to interfere with his work. He is about half way through setting the parts on the garage floor when he senses someone close by. He glances up. Elizabeth is standing about five feet away.

She has a bright smile on her face, warm and inviting. She looks at him admiring his every move. She takes one step closer without uttering a word.

Julien returns her smile with one of his own, passing along his affection to her. He is not surprised she's made a visit. She's done this many times before so that it has almost become a routine part of their secret life together. He welcomes their encounters, yet privately wanting an open relationship. Perhaps one of these days, he confides to himself.

She too has her own hidden secrets of their life together, yet she knows there is only one way to make that happen. Past failures will not deter her from reaching her passionate goals. She is the first to speak. "Good morning Julien. How is your day going?"

It is almost the same greeting each time they meet. He understands why that is. They don't know who might be eavesdropping, and they can not afford to make any mistakes, even after their mission is complete. No one must ever know of their secret love.

"Fine, thanks, and how are you today?" He's said this so many times before it's become mechanical. He'd like to change the words, but they've agreed that the words are only to be changed when there is danger nearby. He sticks to the agreed upon script.

She takes another step closer. His heart takes another beat.

Stranger on a Train

"Is there anything I can help you with?" He stands, arms extended outward.

"Yes there is." She walks towards him.

They hug, holding each other tightly as if this is to be their last embrace.

"I love how you smell in the morning, so fresh. I want to hold you forever."

She smiles, fully aware of her impact on him. While she's grown attracted to him over time, she is not blinded by her true intentions. She is able to keep her role in check. She is that convincing.

"Soon, my love. Soon we will be free to be together as it should be." Her smile does not quite reach her eyes.

They linger in each other's arms for another few seconds until she pulls away, yet still holds onto his hands. Her smile is now full and convincing to him.

"We must find another way. Do you have any ideas?"

Julien answers, "I was convinced this would work. Positive in fact. I'm sorry to have disappointed you."

"Disappointed us," She corrects. "Remember, we are in this together, you and me." She swings their joined arms back and forth in a playful way.

"Yes, but of course." He loves the way she looks. A stray beam of light from the morning's sun shines brightly on the side of her face.

There are a few seconds of silence that is awkward to her, but tantalizing to him.

"Might the young man, Paul, be of any service?" he asks.

95

She gives him a grin. "I've too been thinking about that. I'm not so sure yet. The more people involved the more complex it gets. I feel safe with only you and me." She is unaware of her daughter's exploits with Paul.

"Just an idea."

"Yes, and I appreciate it, but let's wait a while. Something might come up."

They stand still for another few seconds until she goes on. "Do you have time for me?"

His eyes light up.

They head for a small, more private, part of the garage to make love.

Elsewhere, however, Anne is up to something else.

Quietly she makes her way to the bottom of the stairs, waiting just long enough for her father and Paul to leave the house. She looks around to make sure she is alone, knowing she can't be too careful. "Mother?" she calls out, waiting for a signal one way or the other to proceed. There is no response so she advances towards Paul's bedroom, taking one stair at a time. She puckers her lips along the way simultaneously thinking about where her mother might be. Nothing comes to mind.

Now facing the bedroom door, she turns the door handle and pushes. The door easily opens to the pressure. Anne keeps the door partially open so she can hear anyone approaching her location. She heads for the furniture stand to retrieve *Car Maintenance and Repair*, and then stops short when she does not spot the magazine. "Maybe he read it?" she asks herself. She looks around but finds nothing.

Next, she makes her way to the bathroom, thinking he might have read it while he was on the toilet. Again, she comes up empty handed. "One place left," she tells herself.

She moves towards the closet to see if it is there. Nothing, except for his clothes, shoes, and two pieces of luggage she recognizes. About to close the door, she hesitates for a few seconds. Something doesn't seem to be right, the way the items in the closet are arranged. Wrinkles give rise on her forehead as she tries to organize the information. Still, nothing jumps out at her. For the second time, she is about to leave the closet when she spots a crack in the corner of the closet wall. She pulls a chain hanging from the light socket above her head to get a better look. Then she leans closer to the strange crack. Now on her hands and knees, she feels along the wall for nothing in particular, just hoping to find something of importance. Using the palm of her hand, she presses at various spots on the wall's corner and then suddenly the wall gives way. A pressure-sensitive door flips opens. It startles her so she jumps back just staring at her find.

"What the …" She's not sure what she's just found, yet she is taken aback at the revelation. She sticks her head into the opening. "Whew." It smells dusty with stale air. "This must be a tunnel of some sort!"

Anne leans back to rest on her folded legs. She thinks aloud. "I know that a lot of these mansions in this area, way back when, were safe houses for slaves. Not all whites believed in slavery, many tried to keep them alive and well. Could this be one of those secret passages where slaves entered and left this old house?" The mere thought of that possibility bursts in on her in a sudden wave of amazement that takes her breath away. She feels giddy with the prospect of it being true.

Secrets are hard to keep, even for her. She wants to tell someone, yet she is not sure who that might be. Who would also keep it a secret … definitely not her father … her mother might … Paul is a question mark. No one comes to mind that she believes she can trust. She decides to keep it to herself for the time being, and maybe do a little research on her own to get more information about safe houses for slaves.

Neatly, she returns the small door to its original position and leaves the bedroom, still wondering where the magazine might be.

Elsewhere, Elizabeth and Julien lay in each other's arms in silence.

Enjoying the pleasures offered from of one another, Elizabeth and Julien linger in bliss, not wanting the feeling to end. Yet, she is thinking of her next move to put a final end to the turbulent marriage with Marcus. She isn't sure how much longer she can take it. She is uncharacteristically quiet right now. Julien suspects something.

Stranger on a Train

"A penny for your thoughts," he innocently asks, unaware of what he is about to hear next.

She ponders whether to give it all to him or let whatever happens just happen.

"We need each other. You can count on me. You know that, don't you?" He persists. "What's on your mind?"

She rolls over to one side, now facing away from him, not wanting him to see her worried look. She just doesn't know how to say it, so she rumbles some words around in her mind to pick the right ones so that there isn't any misunderstanding. She doesn't think she's even close to scripting the piece properly.

He leans over, gently touches her shoulder realizing something is up, something very important. He knows better not to push her into divulging her thoughts. She doesn't like to be pushed too hard, gently, perhaps, but not in a demanding manner. He's already learned that lesson a while back and intends to remember it. "I'm worried about you. You know you can tell me anything." A troubled look now appears on his face, mirroring in a way, the same expression as hers, yet his voice is soft and reassuring.

She quickly turns his way, almost smacking him in the face. He jumps back just in the nick of time to avoid a mild collision. "Oh, I'm sorry. I didn't mean to startle you." She takes hold of his face with both her hands, caressing him in a gentle-like way.

He covers her hands with his, looking directly into her eyes.

"I've been thinking about what we need … must … do next."

Antonio Vianna

Hoping to make light of a tense situation, he says, "While we were making love?"

"Oh no my love. When we give each other pleasure I'm only thinking of you … of us … together … forever." She seems to be sincere and for the most part she is. However, there is another part of her psyche that lurks in the shadows, a part that can compartmentalize her thoughts and emotions. She strokes his face again giving him the look that he desperately desires from her.

"What is it then? Tell me." His grip on her tightens.

"Well … it's about Paul?" She looks away to conceal any sort of fabrication he might pick up from her.

"Paul. What about him? What does he have to do with anything?" He is genuinely confused.

Continuing facing away she goes on. "I think … believe … Paul can be of assistance to us."

Still not following exactly what she means he presses on. "I'm still not following you."

She turns to meet his eyes. "He can help us put Marcus away for good."

He is motionless and without words.

She helps him out. With a tone of finality she clarifies for him. "I've seen Paul gain the trust of Marcus. All we need to do is convince Paul that he must make Marcus disappear … that it is in his best interest as well." She waits for some sort of reply and when one is not forthcoming she keeps it going. "Marcus may be beginning to suspect something from me … us … and Paul is the obvious decoy. Whatever reason Marcus dreamed up to bring the young man to my home in the first place was just a sham. I'm convinced of that. Marcus had something else in mind. It wasn't about finding what happened to Damien. No. My son was not killed, and Marcus knows that. I believe he wants Paul to do his bidding, to dig up something that will harm me. I think he wants me killed."

Shock fills Julien's face. "Kill you! Why on earth would he want to do that?"

She takes a deep breath before she tells him. "He doesn't have two pennies to rub together. If it weren't for me to subsidize his preoccupations, then his life style would be worthless. In the event that I die before him, everything goes to him, everything!"

"Can't you simply change your will? Allow Anne to inherit your estate. Give it to charity. Let the sunshine state of Florida get it. Do something that puts him out of the picture."

"I wish it were that simple, but it isn't. Believe me, I've tried many times to make the change. We have an irrevocable contract. There is only one way for him not to get anything." Her lies are convincing. The will has been changed long ago.

He finishes her thought, "He must die before you."

"Yes, that sums it up."

"I didn't know."

"Up to now, I hadn't told you."

They look away from each other as if to reset their thinking in a new direction.

Julien is the first to have another idea. "I don't like the idea of bringing another person into our plan. It's too risky." He sees a smile start to glimmer on her face that encourages him to continue. "Whatever role we assign to Paul, he must never know the real purpose. We don't want to be obliging to him or to anyone else."

She likes what she hears, and more importantly proud of herself to have led him into this particular conclusion. There is just one more piece of the scheme that she needs to covertly feed him. "That might be difficult. Remember, he's got the trust of Marcus and we'd have to do something quite dramatic to create a big enough wedge for distrust to seep between them."

"Oh, I see." He pauses, "Anything in mind?" He continues to look serious.

"We don't tell Paul anything."

He frowns, now off track of what she is getting to.

"Both of them would disappear at the same time." Her voice is flat without being emotionally troubled with the plan.

He remains quiet and doesn't answer.

They both look at each other knowing the truth. It didn't work out the way they planned the first time around. They have to be sure this time. There may never be another try at it.

She decides it is best to keep silent as well.

On the surface it seems to be calm and normal, but beneath the façade of serenity is turmoil that not either one had envisioned. The longer they remain still, the greater the anxiety. An invisible mist covers them for a short time, cut off from the horror of their murder scheme. Seconds tick by as thoughts cling to corners of the small room not yet willing to let go.

Stranger on a Train

"I just don't believe it!" It seems so long ago that he was sitting at his computer, alone, working on the next plot of his book. No other worries than to figure out character development and unified scenes. He wishes he were back there now. Life can change so suddenly at times, right before your eyes.

"Believe me or not, I am telling you the truth … voire dire."

This is not what Paul had been expecting to hear. His mind seems to be taking a few short cuts to conclusions he simply does not understand. Further, he is not prepared for what Marcus is about to say next. No one could have predicted it.

"In addition to Anne being behind our near fatal car accident, she is also responsible for Damien's murder. My own daughter …" His voice trails off as if he too is overwhelmed with revelation. He takes a deep swallow of air that nearly results in a dry cough. He seems to believe he knows the truth, but does he really? Is he suppressing what really happened?

"You've got to be kidding." Paul cannot think of anything else to say for the moment.

"I wish it weren't so. That's why I need you so greatly. There isn't anyone else I can turn to, or even trust." His eyes have a desperate look to them as if the words are unnecessary to express his inner turmoil.

Trying to remain rationale, Paul says, "How do you know she was behind the brakes' failure and Damien's disappearance? What ..."

"He was killed!"

"Ok, Ok." Paul puts both hands up, palms towards Marcus to ward him off. Then he goes on. "How do you know she's responsible?"

"I've gone over this before with you. I just know. I know her, what she's capable of. Hell, she's my daughter." He rolls his eyes as if the truth is so obvious that an explanation is not needed, yet it isn't the truth that he tells.

Paul mirrors Marcus's eye movements and whispers to himself, "So be it." Then with a louder voice he says, "Why did you pick me?"

Marcus gives him a frown, unsure of the meaning of the question.

"You only met me for a short time on the train, and that was a while back. Why me? Had you been looking a while for someone to come here but found no one until me? Were you so desperate that I became your last resort? What was it?"

"Why is that so important to you? You're here and that cannot be changed. I'm paying you a handsome wage for your services, more than you've ever made selling your books. You should be thankful that I've come along to rescue you from your pitiful writing existence."

"Pitiful writing existence! You have no right to say that, no right what so ever!"

"I just did and I'll say it repeatedly if I so chose. Don't ever tell me what I can or cannot do, should or should not do. Never! Do you understand me?"

It seems the conversation has moved to a totally different level, hail stones colliding against window panes from all angles, slipping ever so closely to one another yet avoiding direct hits that would bring everything to a final end. The face-off seems as if it will balloon into a confrontation where there will be only one of them left. Neither one seems willing to pull back, to remove the challenge. It is during these instances when a level head is necessary. Who will it be? Seconds tick away.

In the corner of the room the long pendulum of an old grandfather clock gently swings back and forth. Its free swinging motion under the action of gravity regulates it movements.

Tic – tock. Tic – tock. Tic – tock.

The sound from the timepiece takes center stage.

Bong!

The clock announces that it will make known the current time. Fifteen chimes ring out.

The sound is sufficient to break off the stalemate.

Each man gives a silent sigh of relief.

Neither intended to let the conversation ascend to such a heightened level, yet each man was not willing to be the first to give in, a sure sign of weakness. As if on cue, each man steps away from the other as if each needs fresh air to think through his next move. The clock measures the length of the silence with its tic – tocks.

"I still want to know why you picked me … and then waited for such a long time to contact me." Paul waits for a response and when one does not come forth he persists. "I'm not going to let this go. I want to know."

"I'm not particularly pleased with what I'm about to say, but you are persistent, so here it is." He clears his throat as if he is about to address a large audience about something very important. "I was on one of my holidays, just to get away from this place, my family, just for a short time. You can't imagine what it is like to live with these two women."

Paul interrupts, "Your wife and daughter?"

"Who else." He rolls his eyes as if he is looking for some sort of sympathy. "Elizabeth never lets me forget that it is her family's money that supports our life style. If it were solely up to her she wouldn't spend a penny on anything she couldn't get for free, borrow, or steal." Another clearing of the throat separates the next thought from smoothly flowing forth. "I enjoy life. I want to do things, go to places that I've never been to, try out new things. I mean, life is a relatively short journey for each of us. We never really know when it is going to end, and what the final scene will be like. Do you understand what I'm saying?" He looks squarely in Paul's eyes, seeming desperate to get some sort of agreement from the younger man.

Paul is too overwhelmed with Marcus's portrayal of his life to make a response, so the older man continues with a disappointing frown on his face.

"I guess you don't. You're too young to understand the fragility of our lives." He takes in a deep breath and lets the air slowly escape through his nose. A whiff-like sound signals his breathing pattern. "I'm not a real architect … only took a few classes to get a certificate. But I do enjoy structural design and construction of buildings. Do you know Frank Lloyd Wright?" He earnestly waits for an answer.

Not sure an answer is what Marcus is looking for, Paul remains quiet.

"No?"

Recognizing the miscalculation Paul says, "Of course I do … probably the first American architect of world significance … a student of Louis Sullivan from Chicago."

"Very good," he claps his hands, "bravo," and then goes on. "I once visited one of Wright's designs in Bear Run, Pennsylvania … Fallingwater, the Kaufmann House. It is of reinforced concrete, real stone, masonry, steel-framed doors and windows … a splendid respect for natural materials and the relationship between the environmental setting and the structure … simply splendid."

For the first time Paul sees a sincere and happy smile on the face of Marcus. It seems to startle him a bit for some reason, but then he realizes he is witnessing some sort of personal pent up admission from the older man. He decides to listen for more.

"Elizabeth does not appreciate my interests. I often wonder what the original attraction was between us. So long ago, I've forgotten." His voice trails off almost to a whisper. He steps into silence, sort of a brief moment of hibernation. Then he picks up where he left off. "But that was then, and this is now." His voice lifts into a more positive sound. "I found in you someone whom I intuitively believed I could trust. Yes, I know I waited a while before I made contact with you. And yes, I also know I misrepresented to you the reason why I wanted you to come here. I know all of that, and I offer no real explanation. Perhaps, I didn't have enough nerve to follow through sooner. The real point now is that I need you to help me investigate Damien's murder. I know his body was never recovered. I know that. But, you've got to help me." He ends with a pleading like tone, seemingly hopeless in a way to reel in an alliance.

Not sure it is his turn to say something, he moves ahead just the same. "What's behind the locked door near my bedroom?" He is surprised the question results in a sudden shift in the mood.

"Wha – what?"

"I think you know what I'm talking about." Paul believes the conversation has now rotated in his favor.

Marcus looks away, giving himself time to collect his thoughts. "We've put all of Damien's personal belongings in that room. It is locked." He pauses. "You have no need to know anything more, and I ask you to respect my privacy on the matter." A hint of moisture appears at the corner of both eyes. While the tears are real, is the verbal message true?

Paul nods his head affirmatively.

"Be careful of Anne. Like mother, like daughter." This he is convinced of.

Stranger on a Train

The next day, half way through the tutoring session, Anne tells Paul a secret. He is shocked at the news.

"You're not focused today. Is there something else on your mind?" The question, while innocent in nature, is anything but simple. Paul has no idea what is on the mind of Anne, but is soon to find out.

She squirms in the chair, almost childlike, as if preoccupied with playful things she'd rather do at the moment. She thought she'd be able to conceal her discovery in the closet for a much longer period until she had time to think about what her next move should be. However, what she stumbled on is getting the best of her. She can't hold back any longer. "I found something." She looks at him.

Paul gives her a quizzical look, not following her at all.

"I found something in the closet of your bedroom. I'm not sure what it is, but I think it is important."

Paul's perplexed look continues. He wonders why she was in the closet at all, but does not ask right now. He probably should have.

"I think it is some sort of tunnel that leads somewhere I'm not sure. I'm guessing it's been there for quite some time."

The snippets of information only serve to confuse him more. He is not sure what the bits and pieces of seemingly unrelated information has to do with anything. Paul is about to ask her a question but is cut off before he gets out a word.

"I think, although I'm not positively sure, the tunnel leads to the outside and was used to secretly transport people, like slaves, or something else, into this house and then out. I don't think it's been used for a while, but I'm not sure. I mean it might still be used today, right now. I really don't know. I think it is important. I think we should look into it."

"Whoa, wait a minute." He puts his hands up, palms towards her to get her to stop talking. "You're not making sense at all. Start from the beginning."

Her eyes are wide, not from a delightful matter, but rather from a troubling event. She now has reservations whether bringing the subject up with Paul was smart. It's too late; the bird is out of the cage.

"Let's start at the beginning. What were you doing in the closet?"

She definitely realizes she's made a terrible mistake; no doubt now. She might lie about it, say something that casts total absurdity on the situation. She might tell him to forget she brought up the topic; that she doesn't want to talk about it any more. She might tell him a partial truth, that she was snooping around, just curious about him. She might tell it all, trying to retrieve the magazine she left in his room before he arrived at their house. She's not sure what approach might work with the man looking straight at her. Pressure mounts as she tries to figure out what next to do. She clears her throat. "Paul, let's forget about what I've just said. It's really not important, really." She is not convinced this is the right decision, but it's now out there. She waits to see how he grabs hold of it.

He knows she is not telling the truth, so he presses her on the matter. "Anne, I really don't think you want to forget about it. I think there is something you want to tell me. There's more, isn't there?"

Stranger on a Train

The difficulty she had just a few seconds ago to decide what approach to take with him is now a simple matter. No longer consumed with doubt she tells him it all. "You're going to think terrible of me, I'm sure of it."

"Let me decide that. Go on."

"Initially I wanted to get the magazine I left in your room before you arrived, *Car Maintenance and Repair.*"

He interrupts, "I didn't know you were into cars." He is genuinely surprised.

"Yeah, well that's how it is. I have a wide variety of interests."

"What were you doing in the room before I arrived? I mean, don't you have your own bedroom?"

She wiggles her eyebrows which does not make sense to Paul, but that secretly reveals a hint into her sexual fantasies. She is not about to tell him everything about herself, so she gives him a smile that compounds the confusion.

Figuring he just hit a dead end with the question, he says, "Ok, go on."

"But the magazine wasn't there. I figured you took it to read and left it someplace else."

"No. I didn't take it. I don't think I even picked it up."

"Oh." She lifts her hands to cover her mouth.

"Why are you surprised? What else is there?"

Arms still extended to her face, she curls her fingers just enough to expose her mouth. "What do you mean?"

He gives her a grin that is the kind you give someone when you know they are not being honest. Otherwise, he remains silent letting the facial expression tell it all.

Remaining in the same position, she says, "Then someone else took it from your room."

"But who would do that, and why would anybody want the magazine? What is its value?"

"I don't know, at least not now, but I think it is important to find out."

"Why?"

She cocks her head slightly to the left as she shrugs her shoulders. "I don't know yet, call it a hunch." Then she adds, "Remember, I told you I'm psychic."

He lets out a long sigh, and continues. "Ok, so what else is there? The tunnel, what's with the tunnel?"

"So after I didn't find the magazine on the furniture stand where I thought I left it, I began to look around. Went to the bathroom but it wasn't there. Then, went to the closet and couldn't find it there either. But, I saw something strange looking in the corner of the closet so I looked more closely. And, that's when I discovered a sort of trap door and what I think is a tunnel." She pauses. "That's it. Then I left the room."

He stares off into space in no particular place, just letting his eyes drift away to wherever they decide to roam. They finally find a resting location, a wooden leg of chair across the room. Nothing seems to register with him right now, just a pleasant feeling of being at ease. He's not sure how long his mental journey lasted but the trek is interrupted when he hears Anne's voice.

"Anne to Paul, are you in there?"

He comes around with a quick blink of his eyes. "Yes."

"Welcome back."

"Huh?"

"You were someplace else, not here. Now you're returned."

"Oh, I'm sorry. That happens to me at times. I just drift away with thoughts."

She gives him a smile, somewhere between compassion and tolerance with perhaps a little impatience mixed in for good measure. Now, she wants to move on, no longer intent of hiding information from him. She asks him a question. "What do you make of all this, the missing magazine and the tunnel?"

"I'm not sure what there is to make of it. You're the psychic. Remember?"

"Oh, come on Paul. There is something to be made of it. Why would anyone take a magazine from your room? Why would there be a tunnel?"

"Well, I know that many years ago houses like this one were safe havens for slaves …."

She interrupts, "Yes, I know all of that. This might have been one of those tunnels that were used for slaves to enter and exit. I know that."

"But you think there's more to it?"

"Yes, but I don't know what."

"Then there is something you're not telling me. Perhaps there is something you're suppressing into your subconscious that is too scary or hurtful to remember."

"Please, you're a writer, not a psychiatrist."

Antonio Vianna

"Have it your way. But I still think you know more than you realize."

"Maybe so." She has no intention of telling him that experts say she is developing psychometric abilities, which means she will be able to pick up information including images from touching objects or people, even by being touched. Only in its early development phase, she is excited about the prospects. The mere thought of this possibility makes her feel as if she belongs to another world.

He wets his lips, "Can we get back to our studies?" He's forgotten for the moment about the unexpected reappearance of his driver's license.

However, late at night while he is asleep something else takes place.

Damien continues to drink one beer after another. He looks around the littered room inside the barge. It is filled with rubbish and all sorts of other useless trash. He starts to feel sorry for himself, feeling anger grow deep inside. He takes another swig of beer and then for some strange reason spits it out. Most of it lands on his already dirty shirt. His lips don't even want to cooperate with his action, yet the move symbolizes the dismal condition he is in.

He takes the half filled bottle and heaves it towards the opposite wall. The container bounces off without breaking, the result of little propulsion coming from his throw. His strength

114

seems to diminish with increased alcohol consumption. The bottle rolls on the steel floor, clinking and clanking as it moves over rivets that hold the pieces of metal in place. It rests along side other pieces of debris.

He takes in deep breaths and exhales the air. He finds it cumbersome to exercise these simple movements now. He begins to wonder if his own death is near.

Out of the blue, he starts to cry, soft sobs at first that find their way to bawling loudly. The sound from his wailing is unusual to his ears, and in a way very scary. He is unable to control the emotional outburst, so he lets it run its course. It continues longer than he ever expected.

Yet as it seems to end its course, he begins to feel a sense of relief as if a huge load has been lifted off his shoulders. He stays put, not sure what else might unexpectedly come along the way. Then, as quickly as the crying shrieked out, his body starts to tremble. He is now certain the end of his life is at this time. In some ways, he is thankful that all his pain and suffering will come to a conclusion. He wonders what will happen next so he lets go of fighting. He gives in to whatever comes his way.

His shaky body settles down, no longer quivering. He begins to feel good, in fact very good, and wonders if he is hallucinating or, if he is now dead and off some other place, away from an earth bound existence? He has no idea so he waits for a message of some sort to tell him what next to do. The time seems to last a long while, or so he thinks.

There is no confirmation, not even a hint at what is in store for him.

He wonders if he is the experiment, the one being analyzed. Has he been abducted by aliens? Foolish, he shouts silently to himself. Not possible.

Then, he starts to believe it is a test, a sort of trial to assess the next staging. He promises to do his best to pass the examination, but down deep inside questions if he is up to it. He was not good at school tests as a child.

Damien looks around, eyes slowly moving left to right, up and down. He looks for a clue to tell him something. He finds what he is looking for.

Out of the corner of his eye he spots a wallet with several credit cards scattered about. At first he is not sure who they belong to, certainly not his. Then he understands what is going on. He hasn't physically gone anyplace. He's been sitting in the same place all along. He's had some sort of eye-opener to his life. He knows what he needs to do. He readies himself to pay a secretive visit.

He grabs the wallet in his hands. He finds a piece of paper that he tears into a small portion, and then writes a short note that he stuffs into the wallet. He'll turn over the credit cards once he meets Paul face to face, if that should ever happen.

Now, one o'clock in the morning he silently heads for the house, the place where he once lived not that long ago. He goes the same way to the house he previously used, and once there, he crawls through the tunnel to reach his former bedroom. He counts on the fact that Paul is sound asleep before he opens the small door that leads to the closet. His heart is not beating as fast as it did during the prior visit. He can't explain that fact, so he lets the thought fade away.

Stranger on a Train

Once inside the closet he sneaks towards the bed where Paul lies, snoring with every other breath. He looks at the man and wonders who this person really is, hoping that he will have a reasonable good answer some time soon. He has some important stories to tell the man. Damien turns to a furniture stand nearby and pulls out the wallet from his pocket. He places it so that it is easily visible to Paul when he wakes up. He looks around the room at nothing in particular, but he feels a little sadness creeping its way inside him. He's not sure why that is, but he lets it linger as long as possible until it vanishes away. There is some satisfaction associated with the feeling. The job now completed, Damien makes his way back to closet and away from the house.

Within an hour he sits inside the barge, waiting to make the acquaintance of Paul. He soon falls asleep, feeling exhausted, both physically and mentally.

The next morning Paul awakens with a strange feeling overcoming him. He can't figure it out, but considers it might be something he dreamt about last night. It wouldn't be the first time his nighttime dreams linger into the day. Some of his great stories have come from dreams. He gives himself a smile as he stretches his arms above his head. "Ahhhh,' he gives out a sigh.

He moves out of bed, headed for the bathroom to complete his morning routine. Once finished he gets dressed and heads for the door. Out of the corner of his eye, however, he spots something that takes him by surprise. He stops dead in his tracks. He catches a glimpse of his wallet. "What the ..." He moves closer to it for further scrutiny. He can't believe it as he opens the leather accessory. Inside is a piece of paper. He opens the note to read it.

**Meet me outside
The Island Cow on Periwinkle.
Today. Noon.
Come alone.
I'll find you.**

His eyes stay glued to the message. "What's going on?" He checks the other side of the note to find it to be blank. Paul wonders if he should follow the directions or just let it go. That would be the easiest thing to do, just forget about it, or would it. For Paul, probably not. He is too curious to simply let the mysterious communication go unanswered. And definitely, he intends to keep it all secret.

Now firmly settled on a decision he returns the note into the wallet and then he places the wallet into this pants pocket. He heads off to get some breakfast, although all of a sudden he does not feel hungry.

Stranger on a Train

Already finished with most of her breakfast, Anne sips the last remains of coffee. She smiles as Paul approaches. "How did you sleep?"

He thinks there is a deeper question than the obvious. He wonders if Anne is the mystery person who returned his wallet and who wrote the note, so he gives her a grin. "Fine, how was yours?" He moves past her as he talks, headed towards the kitchen to pour a cup of coffee. "Want a refill?" he asks along the way.

"No, I'm full. Been up for a while."

His mind starts to make all sorts of connections that otherwise, under normal conditions, might not make real sense, but these are not normal conditions. He decides to play a little cat and mouse game with her, figuring he can catch her in a lie.

"Ever been to *The Island Cow*?" he asks casually, although he hears his voice quiver slightly. He takes a sip of coffee before refilling it to the rim. He moves towards her in the other room.

"On Periwinkle. It's a fun place. Why?"

"Oh. I've heard about it and I'm just wondering what it's like."

"Maybe we should go there sometime."

"You mean together?"

"That's the idea, you and me."

"Do you have any plans later on today?" He takes a sip of coffee to cover the nervousness he feels inside. A little of the dark liquid slips off the cup's rim before it reaches his lips.

"When is my tutoring session?"

"Ah, yes … the tutoring session."

"That's what I said. When is it?"

Paul hesitates, forgotten about the daily commitment. He frowns.

"You're acting strange this morning. Something is on your mind. Want to share?"

In a low whisper to himself he says, "I bet you would."

"Paul, you are really acting weird right now. What's going on?"

He keeps his eyes focused on her wondering if she is acting or for real. He admits he can't tell the difference right now, so he decides to play it safe. "Our session is later on this afternoon, say at four. I've got some errands to run before then." He hopes he is convincing enough to detour the conversation into something less risky.

She doesn't buy a word of what he says, but does not let on. "That's actually better for me. I want to review some of my reading notes before I discuss them with you." Anne gives him a broad smile that is quite persuasive.

"Good. That's settled." He feels satisfied with his part of the discussion, but in fact, should be worried. He is more transparent to her than he thinks.

"Well, I'm off for a while. Hope you have a good rest of your day, and I'll see you at four o'clock." She stands to leave Paul alone, all along knowing something is up. She's no fool.

Now alone, he assures himself that he can get to the bottom of the mysterious person's actions as well as the person's identity. He has no suspicion that Anne will be tailing him.

Stranger on a Train

The rest of the morning moves along without much incidence, but not fast enough for either Paul or Anne who anxiously wait alone by themselves. It is Paul who makes the first move.

He leaves the house, followed closely by Anne.

Paul waits outside the restaurant, walking back and forth on the dirt parking lot. The day's heat and humidity begin to rise making it a little uncomfortable to keep up the pacing, but continues the movement, too nervous to stay in one place. He looks around to spot someone who might have their eye on him, but comes up empty handed with each glance. He starts to worry that the mysterious person will not show. His throat begins to dry up from the rising outside temperature and the physical exercise.

Anne is hidden at the corner of a large porch where other guests are enjoying their meals. Her spot is a perfect location for spying. She wonders what Paul will do next.

He thinks about giving up the idea when all of a sudden a young boy about ten years old approaches him. Paul stares at the child not sure what the boy wants.

Without saying anything the young boy hands Paul a note and then quickly runs away before Paul can ask a question. The piece of paper is clenched in his right hand.

Antonio Vianna

"Well open it," says Anne just low enough so that only she can hear herself. "Come on, we don't have all day." She feels tension build up inside.

Paul looks down at the paper in his hand as if he just realized its existence. He fumbles to open the note as it slips out of his hand to fall on the dirt. He stares at it.

"Well pick it up. Do I have to do everything for you?" Anne's patience begins to disappear.

Paul kneels to pick up the paper, unfolds it to read the message. It is in the same handwriting style as the first note.

You're being watched.
I'll contact you again.
Try the fried calamari.

Chapter 5

Just to the north of Sanibel Island is Captiva Island, the second, smaller, and more remote of the two barrier islands connected to the mainland of Florida. Upscale accommodations, shopping, dining, and recreation hallmark this island resort.

While you may spend endless time walking the white sandy beaches in search of the right sea shell, not everything is what it seems to be.

Just about a half mile past Buck Key refuge lands, on the west side of the Island across Sanibel – Captiva Road, are magnificent mansions belonging to a diverse group of owners. One such owner is the Order of the Metamere, an organization devoted to self-illumination through spiritual cleansing. The list of followers is kept highly confidential and new membership is only through referral from current devotees. Another key prerequisite for consideration of membership is the person's current financial worth and the estimated financial sustainability. Not everyone who seeks association with the Order is admitted.

Marcus seeks membership to this exclusive organization, yet the odds are against him. He is too dependent on Elizabeth's personal financial well being rather than on his own. He is before the Order's Supreme Board for a review. He pleads his case in earnest.

"You must know my deep commitment to the Order's purpose. I have studied intensely and take the mission seriously."

"Mr. Varro, there is no question of your devotion. The real issue is your lack of personal financial sustainability. To be blunt about it, you don't own much of anything. You're dependent on your wife for everything you do. We are only granting you an interview based on one of our former member's recommendation, who incidentally is deceased. Being before us under your, well, special situation, is highly unusual. I trust you appreciate this."

They both know the truth.

The Board's Chair continues. "However, if you could somehow persuade your wife to pledge herself to our mission, well, that would change the situation immensely. We would welcome both of you with opened arms. Or, should you accumulate sufficient wealth, assets that are yours, not someone else's, again, that might adjust our thinking. I hope I am making myself clear."

"Yes you are. With all due respect, I've tried, but, well, she does not understand. I've tried …." His voice trails off into a whisper that he too cannot hear.

"Yes, we suspected as much." There is a slight pause as the Chair looks to each of his sides at the other Board members sitting nearby. He picks up the silent signal to go on with the final declaration. "We are very sorry to have to declare you ineligible. This is the final review for your case, unless, of course, something of importance should change."

Marcus drops his head, embarrassed by what he already knew to be the decision before he actually heard it said aloud. He slowly rises and leaves the room in defeat for the time. He is already thinking ahead how to create an important change the Board seeks.

Why is Marcus so intent on being a member of a spiritual organization that in reality is invisible to others? He knows of no worthy community causes the Order supports, only that it portends to change the inner self of its members through its doctrine. Is that what he is really in search of, or is there something else? Is he really not interested in at all in being a better, more enlightened person or just someone who is perceived by his peers to be that way? Is that what he is all about, show and image, but without substance?

Desperate men do desperate things under desperate conditions. Is this one such instance where Marcus has to act in a violent and reckless manner? He thinks through some options, careful not to overlook anything. He wonders if the young man who is tutoring his daughter and assigned to his son's investigation might be of use. There is one way to find out.

The drive through the two tiny islands of Captiva and Sanibel is purposely slow. Traffic speed is reduced by strict enforcement of a reduced speed limit. Various stop signs slow down traffic. Narrow single one-way roads create further speed limitations. None the less, Marcus tries to maneuver as best he can.

There is an upside of slow moving traffic; an opportunity to think about all sorts of things. Is he really trying to come to grips with Damien's loss, not accepting the truth that his son took off to get away from him, not for any other reason? Will Marcus ever accept that he was the cause?

There wasn't a death or a killing in the physical sense, only in the relationship between the father and son. Yet, there was another killing that haunts the Varro family.

And, there is more Marcus is not yet ready to accept.

While his son showed promise of being a professional pianist, Marcus became jealous of the relationship Damien had with his teacher, Alfred. The three of them argued constantly about teaching methods, yet Marcus himself had no such experience in the profession. As the relationship between Damien and Alfred grew, jealously and rage from Marcus also swelled but at a faster pace.

One afternoon, half way through a music lesson Marcus barged in interrupting what was an otherwise productive session. Marcus accused the teacher of manipulating his son, screaming at the top of his lungs that Alfred was plotting to ruin the father – son relationship. He ranted and raved for several minutes, eyes bulging from their sockets, saliva spewing from his mouth with every word. He appeared incoherent most of the time, yet did not let up on the jumbled talk. At one point he charged Alfred with smearing his own personal character. There seemed to be no limit to what Marcus believed Alfred was engineering.

Both student and teacher were taken by surprise. The alleged manufacture of a scheme by Alfred was too preposterous to let alone, so he took up a countering yelling match with Marcus as Damien silently watched.

Hidden outside the room a young girl sat, curled up and frightened from the goings on in the other room. Edna, the youngest of the three children began to cry, first as a soft weep and then into a much louder howl. Her tiny voice, yet piercing in pitch, caught the attention of Damien. He knew the owner of the sound, so he called her name.

Upon hearing her own name from her older brother she rushed to Damien's side, longing to be safe in his arms.

However, the yelling match between Marcus and Alfred was now at much higher stakes. A fist fight broke out.

As Edna entered the room, Marcus threw a vase Alfred's way. Miscalculated with poor judgment the vase hit the young child in the head. She toppled over; blood seeped through her short reddish hair. Quietness took over and everyone froze in place for a few seconds. Then Damien scampered to his sister's side. By the time young Edna was rushed to a nearby hospital she was dead.

Marcus had some explaining to do with the police, but it was more difficult to face Elizabeth and Anne, who had not witnessed the situation. When it was all said and done, his wife and two children did not forgive him, even to today. The police investigation closed the case stating it to be an unfortunate and accidental death thanks to some significant financial contributions from Elizabeth to the Sanibel Police Department that today she earnestly regrets having done. Damien's private music lessons ended when Alfred was dismissed. Life was never the same for everyone.

Today, Marcus feels the blame for killing his own daughter, yet cannot quite put into perspective his son's going away soon after the incident. Why can't he resolve in his own mind these interconnected events? Is the truth too frightening for him to accept; does he believe there is no real cure?

While the piano still remains in the house where it had always been, Edna's bedroom, at the top of the stairs near the room where Paul sleeps, is cut off from the rest of the house. It is not as otherwise proclaimed the space where Damien's personal belonging are kept.

It seems each family member has their own recollection of past events. Is that because each has found an emotional safe place in each of their mind? Will the real truths ever be known and accepted by the Varro family? What will Paul's role be, if he is even able to survive through it all?

Up ahead in downtown Sanibel is a popular restaurant, *The Island Cow*. A unique combination of great food with a fun atmosphere, the place is usually packed to capacity. Vehicles pull in and out of the dirt driveway kicking up dust along the way. Customers run across Periwinkle Way, either racing toward the restaurant to secure a sought out seat, or else leaving the place as they hold onto take-out specials or doggie bags as if the contents within the containers were pure gold bars.

Marcus feels his nerves tighten realizing there is no other option but to slow down. He lifts his foot off the accelerator with much reluctance. He turns his thought to the present for the moment.

A particular pedestrian catches his eye for some reason, perhaps because he is walking along the roadside in the same direction of traffic. He can't figure out if the person is a local or a tourist. However, he is dressed in shabby looking clothes and seems to be teetering left and right. Marcus wonders if the man is inebriated, so he slows his vehicle to be on the safe side. Now about twenty yards from the walker Marcus decides to announce his presence … he hits the vehicle's horn twice with the palm of his hand.

The noise surprises the person on foot. His body jerks in the direction of the road. Marcus slams on his breaks to avoid hitting him, but is not quick enough. Both vehicle and person collide with the metal object winning the battle.

Marcus yells out a profanity, "Shit head," and begins to pound the steering wheel. Traffic behind him comes to a standstill. He starts to get out of the car to check out the condition of the person when a hand appears on the right side of the vehicle, near the right headlight. Marcus continues moving towards the front of the car to get a closer look. Before he is able to get a glimpse of the person's face, the young man scampers across Periwinkle Way into a clump of bushes.

"Hey, come back." Marcus's call is insincere and without much enthusiasm, secretly satisfied that the situation has resolved itself. There is no way to recognize the man, who in reality is his son, Damien.

Then he looks at the place where the car and man met hoping to find no damage. "Great," he says to himself. Without any signs of having a run in, he does not intend to report the incident to his insurance company or to the police.

He turns towards the other vehicles still at rest behind him and shrugs his shoulders. He raises his arms above his head.

Soon after, he is driving back to his house, planning on a meeting with Julien.

Elizabeth turns to him, "I really must go now. I've been gone too long as it is." She sighs with disappointment that satisfies him to no end.

Realizing he too has things to do today, he warmly smiles at her, "I know. Soon we'll not have to be secret about all of this."

"Yes," she reassures him with a grin of her own.

A few minutes later Julien is left alone to work out some things in his head.

Stranger on a Train

She reaches her place just in time to meet Anne who also is returning from a secret rendezvous of her own, yet only as an observer.

"Dear, can I have a word with you?"

Her mother's voice sounds a little different, yet Anne is not sure what to make of it. She seems to be in quite a happy mood.

"I have something very important to tell you, and you must swear to me you'll keep it secret." Now her mother's voice is completely different than just a short time ago. Is her mother in some sort of trouble?

"Yes, of course. What is it? Are you in trouble?"

Elizabeth takes her daughter's face in her hands, caresses the smooth skin in a way only a mother can do. Her smile tames the terror in her daughter. "No. Oh no, quite the opposite. I am in a delightful place and couldn't be much happier. Well, perhaps a little happier. There's always room for more happiness." She tries to make light of what she is about to share with her daughter.

Anne waits, not fully convinced of the mood being portrayed. Her wait is not long.

"We, you and me, need an alliance with Paul." She pauses to let the statement settle in.

Anne is not quite sure what it means, so she keeps silent to let her mother continue. Her mother's touch causes a quick vision to appear, too vague to interpret but enough to make her feel uneasy.

She begins to spin a lie. "For some time now I have believed your father to be unfaithful to me."

Anne lets out a sigh. "And …?"

"Yes, he has." She lets the untruth hang around for a short time before going on. "I hired a private investigator to prove one way, or another, my suspicions. That's where I've just come from, a meeting with the investigator. He showed me photos." She puts her hands to her face to cover the fake embarrassment.

The move does not work. Anne is suspicious but does not let on. She decides to go along to see how far her mother intends to take the tale. She figures there is something in it for her, so she does not interrupt. She gives her mother one of her fake frowns that seems convincing.

"I know this must be a shock to you, but I had to know. I really did. You understand, don't you?"

Anne nods her head to agree not sure speaking anything serves any purpose right now.

"I am overwhelmed with pain. My own husband, the man who …." She decides not to finish the sentence, thinking the dangling thought to be more definitive.

Anne thinks to herself that her mother is real good at this game, something she knows she's learned well herself, from her mother. She thinks she can outsmart the teacher. "I'm so sorry, mother. I had no idea."

The sympathetic words seem to be genuine to Elizabeth, but she wonders. Too late now, she must move forward. "I'm at a lost at what to do. I mean, do I confront him with the truth? I really don't know."

Anne knows her mother well enough that a plan is about to be revealed. Her mother is not known for being at a loss for anything. She continues with a concerned appearance. "Divorce him."

That exact response is exactly what Elizabeth was hoping for. "Yes, that would certainly free me, us, up. However, I think there might be something else. I'm madder than you can imagine. I want him to pay for his infidelity." She seems genuinely getting worked up. "You know I've changed my will to leave him very little, but you with the bulk."

Anne nods a yes figuring saying anything right now might ruin the situation.

"What do you have in mind? How can I help? We're in this together, you and me."

Elizabeth gives her daughter another smile. "Well, there is Paul."

She is startled by her mother's comment, furrows show on her forehead. She is unsure what to make of the comment.

"I think we can form an alliance with Paul. I think you can convince Paul to join us."

"An alliance to do what … what do you have in mind?"

"To get rid of your father, once and for all."

The plan's straightforwardness shocks Anne. She realizes her mother wants her to convince Paul to kill her father. She is not ready for it. She remains silent.

Elizabeth recognizes Anne's reaction. She too might have responded similarly, then again, perhaps not. She needs to get her daughter on board immediately without any hesitation or equivocation. If she waits too long, Anne might back out. It's now or never, so she goes for the jugular. "Do I need to remind you that your father killed your younger sister Edna and caused your brother Damien to run away? You haven't forgotten the suffering he's caused all of us. Now, he's been unfaithful to your mother. What next? What has he done to you that I don't know about? I've had it with him. He's through and I don't want his useless life around me any longer. I want him dead!" She pauses. "There, I've said it. I want him dead?"

"Oh." That's about all Anne can think of saying. Yet secretly she knows the family's turmoil was bound to lead to something like this sooner or later. It is enough, however, because her mother has not yet finished.

"Paul is the only one who can help us. And you are the only one who can persuade him. It's up to you, dear … up to you."

"What exactly is Paul's role? Do you want him to commit the murder?"

The conversation now appears to be between two women planning a party, whom to invite, what food and beverages to order, and the like. It seems all so casual and orderly.

"No, Paul does not need to know the exact details. All you need to do is convince him to play along with whatever our ultimate plan is. For starters I've been thinking about another car accident when he and Marcus are together. But, that's not final. I want to hear from you, your ideas. We're in this together. Like mother, like daughter."

This is nothing like Anne had figured would really happen. Yet, she seems predisposed to agree. However, she has some other ideas that she'll keep to herself for the moment. She has a plan of her own. Like mother like daughter, she silently says to herself with a grin. "Count me in. Just give me some time to snuggle up to Paul. He's not the type of guy whom I had expected to tutor me. I wonder about his sexual experiences. I don't think he's much experienced."

"But you can certainly change that."

"Certainly. You've got to do what you've got to do."

Marcus hurries to get out of the car, intent to talk with Julien about his plans. However, first, upon entering his home he walks directly to a well stocked cabinet of various alcohols. He grabs a bottle of DIMPLE Scotch, golden wire still webbed around the glass container. Placing his fingers in the depressions that give the scotch its name, he unscrews the cap and pours himself a hefty shot. With one swallow he downs the liquid. He savors the taste of good booze, giving out a sigh of satisfaction. Without much thought he pours himself a second round and then heads for his favorite chair. He plops his tired body into it. Now comfortably seated he starts sipping the scotch, just enough to touch his lips each time. The effects of the alcohol seem to settle him down.

His mind starts to roam aimlessly, nothing specific for any measurable length of time, just one snap shot to another. He is not able to connect the individual images. He doesn't seem to care one way or another, so he lets it go on for another minute or so. Is his life flashing in front of him, trying to give him a message or some sort of lesson he should have learned along the way, or, are these simply random thoughts that have

Antonio Vianna

no relationship to much of anything. It is probably not the
later, such as when your computer takes a few moments to load
various programs before you can start its operation; there is a
reason. However, he's not sure nor does he seem to care right
now so he does not push towards concluding anything. He
takes another sip of scotch, and feels weary. He gently rests the
glass on a nearby stand and then closes his eyes. He starts to
breathe deeply and soon is asleep. He begins to dream.

"What are you doing here?"
The sound of the voice is not familiar.
Marcus remains quiet, unable to see.
"I've asked a question, and I demand an answer."
He rubs his eyes,
thinking the move will give him a clear view.
He is startled at what he sees.
_"Ah!"_
The creature asks a question.
"Who were you expecting?"
He is frightened as the figure steps closer.
The voice now sounds creepy.
"Did I send for you, or have you come on your own?"
Marcus is not sure what to say.
He just wants to leave, but is immobile.
The creature is terrifying looking.
Eyes bulge from their red sockets.
Teeth are jagged and crooked.
Skin is scaled and naked.
Fingers and feet are clawed.
A long tail swings back and forth.
Several skulls are atop the creature's head.
The creature steps closer.

136

Stranger on a Train

It reaches out to touch Marcus.
"Come with me."
Marcus resists.
"Oh, no! You're the devil!"
The creature grins.
"Call me Lucifer."
He laughs in a throaty high pitched sound.
Suddenly, smaller devils appear around him.
Marcus screams.
"Don't take me! I beg of you!"
The devil cries out in celebration.
"I am the Prince of Hell!"

Marcus wakens, perspiration clings to his forehead. He is not sure where he is, so he closes his eyes, hoping the move will reset his thoughts. His mouth seems unusually dry so he smacks his lips. With his eyes still shut, he takes deep breaths in and out to settle down his breathing. Soon he feels calmed down and readies himself to look around.

Standing before him is Elizabeth and Anne. They stare at him not sure what to make of it, so they say nothing.

Surprised by their presence, he's not prepared to say much, so he too keeps quiet.

Elizabeth breaks the silence. "What happened? You gave out an eerie scream as if you've seen a ghost or something. Are

Antonio Vianna

you Ok?" She seems genuinely concerned about her husband's well being in spite of the plan that is brewing.

He is embarrassed, not quite sure what the dream was about, so he shrugs it off. "Just a bad dream, that's all. Really nothing, I suppose." He clears his throat.

Elizabeth and Anne remain standing for a little while longer.

"Can I get you something ... a glass of water, perhaps?" Ann asks, also appearing sincere considering her most inner thoughts.

"No, no. I'm alright ... just a bad dream." He waves them away with the palm of his hand.

"As you wish," Elizabeth says. "Come, let's leave your father alone." The two women leave Marcus by himself.

Now by himself again, he looks around and spots the whiskey glass nearby. It seems there is another gulp left so he reaches for it to finish off the remains. The liquid slides down his throat without any problem. He gets off the chair for a refill all the while trying to recall the dream. The recollection is useless, so he resigns himself to forget about it. There are more important things to worry about presently.

"Paul," he yells out the young man's name. There is no answer. He gives it a second try with the same result. He figures he'll have to wait a while. He is interested in an update from the young man about the tutoring sessions, among other topics. He moves back to his favorite chair to resume thinking.

About an hour later, Marcus hears the front door open. "Paul, is that you?"

"Yes it is."

"Wonderful. Please join me in the drawing room."

Soon the two men are face to face.

"I've just had a wonderful meal at *The Island Cow*. Ever been there?"

Not much interested in chit chat, Marcus says, "Yes, but I have more important things to talk with you about. Care for a drink?"

Paul recognizes the brush off. "No thanks. I'm fine."

"Let's move outside where we can talk privately." Marcus lifts his body off the chair. "Follow me."

Now in a back yard garden where no one can overhear their conversation, Marcus begins. "Have you thought any more about my conversation with you about my wife and daughter?" The message is without any emotion. He looks directly at Paul, holding the tumbler of scotch in one hand, steady as a rock.

There is a worried look on Paul's face. "I'm not sure I understand."

"You don't remember that I confided in you?"

Still a little hazy on exactly what Marcus means, Paul is about to ask a question when he is interrupted. "I told you that I believed Anne was behind our near fatal accident and Damien's murder. I also told you about Elizabeth and me, our financial arrangement. Do you remember now?" His voice, while quietly spoken has intensity about it.

"Yes, yes, I remember. But what did you expect me to do with that information?"

"You agreed to start investigating Damien's murder."

"Well, yes, but that was just a short time ago. Really, Marcus, I haven't had much time to get into that."

Marcus gives him a skeptical look. "You better start finding the time."

Paul feels a weight placed on his shoulders, the heaviness beginning to cause some stress and strain. He really wants out of the whole situation but knows that might be nearly impossible, so he shifts the topic to something else. "Don't you want to know how Anne's tutoring is coming along?"

"No, not really. I'm sure everything is fine. Just remember our little arrangement. I want to see some progress."

Marcus walks away before Paul can respond, on to another meeting. He leaves the glass on an empty stand.

In another part of the expansive back yard, Julien waits. He fidgets, not sure why he's been summoned without much notice. He wonders if Marcus suspects his intimate relationship with Elizabeth. He hopes not, but is not certain, so he decides to be on his toes. He starts pacing, anxiety rising with each passing moment. Then, he hears footsteps and looks up to see Marcus approaching.

"Sit down. I have something important to talk with you." Marcus takes a seat on a wooden bench. He faces Julien. "Let me get to the point quickly."

Julien swallows deeply, now convinced he's been caught.

"We've known each other for quite some time."

Julien wonders if a response is in order, but is not sure, so he keeps quiet.

"I've entrusted you with taking care of certain things that are dear to me. I trust you. I hope you trust me." It appears he is looking for some sort of acknowledgment from Julien this time.

"Yes … certainly." That's the best he can muster up at the moment.

"I need your assistance even more now than ever before. Will you help me? I will pay you handsomely."

To Julien's ears it seems more of an order than a request, so he nods his head in the affirmative.

"Good, I knew I could count on you."

Julien's heart starts to race, not sure what next is to come. He's certain that his secret with Elizabeth is not jeopardized, but he senses there is some sort of danger ahead. He can only wait to hear what Marcus has to say.

"I want you to take care of Elizabeth." The words are flat and without emotion.

Antonio Vianna

Julien is not sure what he means. Could it be that Marcus is divorcing Elizabeth and he wants him to pay attention to Elizabeth in his absence? Is that it? He is without words.

Marcus goes on. "I've had it with her, and I want her to be out of my sight once and for all. I don't care how you get rid of her, I just want it done. Hire someone to kill her if that's what it takes. Don't make it messy. I'd rather it not be done on this property, someplace else. She'd have to be lured away somehow. I don't care. I really don't." The words are in a rambling fashion, not well joined together, yet they make sense to Julien. He is shocked.

"You … you want your wife killed?" He can't believe he is saying it aloud.

"Exactly. I want her killed."

The air suddenly feels heavy, suffocating Julien that he finds it difficult to breathe. He coughs.

"I know this surprises you, perhaps even upsets you, but you are the only one I can turn to."

Somehow Julien summons up enough energy to have a logical come back. "I never realized you two were having problems. Everything appears so normal with you."

"Looks are deceiving."

"I guess so." He pauses for a few seconds and then goes on. "Have you thought about going to a marriage counselor to work things out?"

Marcus gives off a smirk that tells it all.

"Ok, then, what about a separation or a divorce." He thinks his voice sounds even but is not sure.

"A divorce would leave me financially broke. She's got all the money. I'm, well, sort of living off her." He bobs his head several times. "She has to be dead for me to inherit her money. It's all spelled out in her will." He really doesn't know the truth of the matter.

"I can't do this, no, I can't. This is not right." His voice is now strained and his eyes look worried. Has he forgotten about the deal he's already made with Elizabeth?

"You can't let me down. You've got to do it."

"No … not me." He hesitates. "Just wait a while. Think about what you're planning to do. This is all wrong. Give yourself more time to think about ways to work this out without killing her." There is another hesitation. "You'll never get away with it. It's rare that these crimes go unsolved."

Marcus stares at the man in front of him, eyes sorrowful with a mix of anger and desperation. He knew asking Julien to commit the murder was a long shot, but he had to try. Who else could he ask? He has no reason to believe Julien will share the information with anyone … yet he should.

The quietness is interrupted by a nearby noise. A watering canister topples over, kicked by someone who had wandered innocently close by. Paul runs away, fleeing as quickly as possible. He can't believe what he's overheard.

Marcus and Julien stare at each other, not sure what to make of the sound.

Julien starts to move in the direction of the tumbling container but is called back when Marcus says, "Probably a stray cat … nothing more."

The look on Julien's face, however, tells another story. He's not so sure. There haven't been many cats in the area that he can remember, but still, he has no other plausible explanation. He steps forward with only one pace and stops. Perhaps he doesn't want to know the truth.

"We're alone ... don't worry." Marcus appears more confident than he really is, but there is no sense passing on his doubt. With a wave of his hand he motions for Julien to come closer to him. He wants to give him one more opportunity to reconsider. In a hushed voice he says, "Elizabeth is worth millions, and I'm currently spending it as if it were mine. I suspect she is about to cut me off, limit me in some way, but I'm not sure exactly what she has in mind." He smacks his lips and then goes on. "If she were to die, everything would be mine, and I would give you enough money to start your own luxury car repair shop that you've talked with me about." He leans closer to Julien, and places a hand on his shoulder. "Just think of it ... your own shop ... with your name. Isn't that what you want?" He hesitates just long enough in the hope that all of this is sinking in. "And it can be yours. I guarantee it. All yours with no strings attached. Isn't that what you really want?" His look is earnest enough, and his voice is certainly believable, yet the message is not persuasive enough for Julien.

He shakes his head, "Mr. Varro I can't do that."

Feeling outrage build up inside, Marcus has the urge to physically get tough with the man, yet he realizes he is not up to it. Julien would most likely overpower him within seconds of any scuffle. He needs another tactic, something else that is fool proof, but what is it?

"I understand. Maybe I'm off my rocker, paranoid about this whole thing, suspecting she is going to let me hang out to dry. I just might need a little rest away from this place to get a clearer perspective. Yes, perhaps that's just what I need to do." Marcus lets the words drift towards Julien wanting him to interpret the message in a sympathetic way.

However, Julien is wiser than Marcus's assessment, but he has no intention to let on. "Good idea, Mr. Varro. You've been working hard these past months, and a little holiday by yourself might be the proper medicine. We all have thought about doing in someone at one time or another. A good rest is what you really need." He is impressed with the delivery, more than he thought he was capable of doing. Confident he has side stepped the issue, he waits for a reply.

"Agreed." Marcus extends his hand for a shake. "You're a good friend to have listened to my nonsense. Can we keep this little discussion just between the two of us?"

Julien reciprocates by extending his hand, "Of course … just between you and me."

Each man knows the other is lying, but does not let on. Other plans need to be hurriedly put in place. Time is running out.

Elsewhere inside the house, Paul is frantic.

Paul's face is distraught, looking older than his natural age. He seems to have aged mightily since just a few minutes ago. The conversation he's just overheard is too much of a shock for him to fully grasp, yet he knows it isn't good. He starts to wonder about his employer's mental state of mind. He flashes to their first conversation on the train, followed by the strange letter he was sent, the change of reasons why he was asked to come here, a suspicion that Anne is responsible for the brake failure and Damien's death, and now the intention to murder Elizabeth! What is going on in this house, this place that seems to be occupied by a strange and unusual family? He wants to shut it out, all of it, to go back to his own place where writing consumed his otherwise normal life. He covers his ears with his hands as if the movement will take care of everything.

Standing still, he feels a little dizzy as if the wind was just knocked out of him. In a way, it has, but more than just the wind. He begins to settle down, now planning a way to leave without anyone knowing. Once his hands drop to his sides he hears his voice called out. He turns in the direction of the sound.

"Paul, what is it? You don't look well." Anne walks towards him.

Unexpectedly, without much warning, he extends his arms her way. He is in dire need of comfort. She fits the bill.

Anne advances faster than she had otherwise intended. His condition seems too grave to let another second pass. She clutches him and pulls Paul close to her body. An eerie image flashes before her that she can't quite make out. Her psychometric powers are still in their infancy. The heat from each other feels good. They are each satisfied but for very different reasons. They remain embraced for a while in silence. It seems exactly what is needed.

She starts to caress the nape of his neck with a free hand. The soothing feels good to him, as she whispers, "It's going to be Ok. Just take it nice and easy."

He feels the warmth from her breath drift into his ear, and begins to settle down. He continues holding onto her as if his life depended on it. However, he should be careful. Things are not what they seem to be.

While she wants to find out what is really going on, she is not sure how long the hugging should continue. There is no rule of thumb in these types of situations, so she keeps him close to her body hoping he makes the next move.

Although he doesn't want to let go, he drops his hands to her waist and gently pushes away. Once separated, he second guesses the decision, but it is now too late. He remains quiet, looking into her eyes that seem so full of beauty. However, the loveliness that he perceives can become a disadvantage to him if he isn't careful. Some gorgeous women use their beauty to manipulate others.

Anne senses it is her turn to take the lead, so she says, "What happened? You can tell me." Her tone is soft and reassuring. She waits knowing her physical attraction is about to start to work.

"I … I overheard something that I can't believe. I mean, I … I just don't believe it, but I heard it."

She wonders if he too realizes he's not making much sense. She gives him one of her award winning smiles and gently

Antonio Vianna

moves her pelvis against him. She feels his immediate reaction to the pleasure, a boon to her ploy.

For a short second he forgets about much other than the sensation he feels. Then, he quickly moves back just enough to change his mood. He feels his body heat up, suspecting the skin color on his face has changed to a slight shade of red.

She comforts him, "Don't be embarrassed. I know." She understands the effect she has on most men and is proud of it. It has given her what she's wanted, for the most part. Still, at the same time, timing is everything so she decides to back off for now. There's enough mojo in her reserve tank to take care of things later on. Further, what's really on her mind is the reason for Paul's anxiety. That takes precedence over her sexual prowess right now. She can't afford to scare him off. She has important plans for him.

He continues to be embarrassed, not having had to deal with a woman like Anne before, beautiful, bold, and confident. In a way, down deep inside, he likes it, but for now the experience is unsettling, too new to get comfortable with. Later on might be another story. He gives in to her reassurances.

Both are relieved that the mood is changing to something else less threatening. She waits for him to say something, hoping no further encouragement is needed.

"I need to sit down. Come on over here." He takes her hand and heads for nearby chairs. "I feel I can trust you, so you have to solemnly promise me you'll not share this with anyone." He stares at her, "Promise me."

Stranger on a Train

She nods her head with a yes, knowing all along she might not keep the commitment.

"Ok, here goes. I know you won't believe me, but you have to."

Anne wants to scream at him to get on with it. Her impatience with his pubescent-like behavior at times challenges her temperament. Yet, she waits to hear him out.

"I was just taking a casual walk through the garden in the back yard, admiring the flowers and such, you know, just breathing in the fresh air."

She silently pushes him to get on with it.

"All of a sudden I heard voices. At first I couldn't make out who they were from, but after I stopped, I was certain your father and Julien were talking."

Anne is stymied why he is taking so long to get to the point. Perhaps, because he is a writer, he feels compelled to layout the context of the situation. Whatever, she takes in a deep breath, all along making him believe she is giving her utmost attention.

"Yes, I was convinced they were talking." He takes a swallow, thinking how good a cold glass of water might taste right now, but he moves on. "So, I listened. I mean, I wasn't trying to eavesdrop, but, well, I was right there and didn't want to interrupt their conversation."

Anne thinks of asking him why he just didn't turn around and leave. The fact is he was overhearing a private conversation, no two ways about that. She resists the question and remains quiet.

"I was close enough to hear what they said to each other. It seemed that your father wanted Julien to do something that he was opposed to. At first I couldn't figure out exactly what that was, but as they continued talking, I knew." He looks away for a short second and then back to Anne.

She thinks his face has become ashen, worried about something very important that is about to be said. She feels some tension build up inside anticipating his next comments, but is shocked at what he tells her.

"They argued back and forth, your father getting quite pushy, and Julien getting quite defensive." He takes in a deep breath.

Anne thinks the real punch line is about to be made, the main point of the entire conversation, so she keeps her eyes on him with a slight smile of encouragement. She whispers to herself, "Go on," so that she is the only one who knows what she is thinking.

"Your father asked Julien to kill your mother. There, I've said it." He tightens the muscles around his mouth to keep it shut. A blank look now appears on his face. He hears no sound around him.

Anne reflects a similar expression found on Paul's face. At first she too is taken back. Then, the empty feeling quickly turns into fury. "That bastard!"

The sudden burst of rage takes Paul by surprise. His body jerks.

"If it weren't for my mother, he'd be peddling pieces of crap on street corners. Are you sure you heard him correctly?" Her look is menacing and it frightens Paul.

Stranger on a Train

"Ye … yes. That's what I heard." His voice is weak and high pitched.

"What did Julien say? Did he agree?" She keeps Paul in her line of sight.

"No … no. He said he couldn't do it … that maybe what he needed was some sort of marriage counseling. That killing his wife wasn't the answer to any problems they might be having."

"What else did you hear?" She has no intention of letting Paul leave without listening to it all.

"You father said he would buy Julien a car repair shop of his own. That he … your father … would inherit a lot of money through your mother's will."

"What else? There's got to be more." She is almost yelling at him at this point.

"I … I don't know."

"You don't know?"

"I … I left, ran away. I was so shocked."

Anne thinks to herself how weak Paul appears right now, a feeble attempt of a real man. She pinches her lips tightly to prevent her from saying what's really on her mind. Then she turns away, just so slightly to look at something other than the person in front of her. She needs to collect her thoughts and get back to the sympathetic and understanding person she wants to portray to Paul. The transformation is made quickly.

"I'm sorry that I got so upset with you. You really took me for a loop." Her voice is now mellow sounding.

Paul does not recognize the sudden mood swing, too focused on himself at the moment. He automatically nods his head to agree with her assessment. He'd like to give her a supportive smile but somehow can't make it happen, so he stares at her without much apparent emotion.

She intends to down play the episode between her father and Julien, but not entirely cast away all worry. If she can make Paul think of even a slight possibility that her father is a dangerous man by creating a wedge of suspicion, she'll have accomplished her intention. "If the truth be known, my father has had bouts with depression. He takes a ton of pills to keep it under control as best he can." She rolls her head from side to side. "He's never come close to harming anyone, just a lot of bluster that's never materialized. I know he's a little strange and all, but I don't think he meant anything he said." She pauses for just the right effect, "Do you?" She gives him a little smile that is something between a happy face and one of worry.

Furrows now appear on his forehead that heretofore had not been visible. He's just not sure what to make of it all. He looks at her in silence.

She gets up from the chair to move close to him. Now kneeling at his knees, she slowly places her face in his lap and lets out a fake whimper. The act works as he gently runs his fingers through her hair. "Let's just keep this between us for now. Ok."

With her face still hidden from him, she gives herself a complimentary grin.

He says, "Yes, I agree. Just keep this between us."

Chapter 6

Later in the evening as everyone is asleep in the house, Damien makes his way through the tunnel for an unexpected visit to Paul. He is surprised at what he finds.

With the trap door now opened, Damien carefully crawls out onto the closet floor. He's sure what he wants to talk about with Paul, he only hopes Paul will listen and believe him. Now standing in the closet he quietly opens the single door, pushing it with the palm of his hand.

He steps into the bedroom, now directly facing the bed. Although the room is dark he can make out a body in the bed, figuring it to be Paul. He takes a step closer and then stops in his tracks. He gives himself a big grin.

Paul has given in to the inevitable.

"Well, well," he says just below his breath, shaking his head from side to side.

He backs off to head towards a chair just a few feet away. He plops his body in it all along thinking what he should do next. Should he awake his sister and Paul, congratulate them on something, or should he just wait it out to see what happens next? He's not sure. He takes a few minutes to think about it, but doesn't have to wait long when one of the two people moves.

Paul quietly leaves the bed to head for the bathroom, presumably to take a pee. He does not notice Damien still seated in the chair. The dark room keeps hidden the unannounced guest. Damien waits for Paul to finish his business and once out of the bathroom, Damien decides to make his move.

"Pss," Damien calls out just loud enough for Paul to hear.

Paul stops in his tracks and listens again.

"Pss, over here," Damien says. He waves his hand ever so slightly to attract Paul's attention.

Paul looks towards Damien. "What the ..."

"Shh, be quiet. We don't want to wake Anne." He puts his index finger to his lips. "Come over here. I need to talk with you."

Paul does not move, still confused on what is going on. He glances towards Anne who appears sound asleep.

Damien now rethinks his plan ever so slightly and gets up from the chair.

Paul backs up a step not sure what is going on.

Damien moves towards the bathroom. "It's more private in here. This won't take long."

Paul hesitates before following.

Soon both men are inside the bathroom, door closed. A small night light dimly shines near the toilet.

"Who are you and what are you doing here?"

Stranger on a Train

"I'm Damien Varro. I was the one who took your wallet, then returned your driver's license, and tried to arrange a meet with you. The last part didn't work out. My sister was following you."

Paul scans the man in front of him, mystified by it all. He keeps quiet.

"I know this is all pretty strange, but you've met a very strange family. Trust me."

Paul spurts out the only idea that comes to mind, "I thought you were dead."

"No such luck. Been in juvenile, at times worse than death, but I'm alive. Want to touch me to make sure?" He extends his arm and lets out a little laugh that sounds eerie to Paul.

"No thanks, I believe you. But I'm confused, what do you want?"

"Let me make this real quick before she wakes up." He motions with his head the direction of Anne. "There are some things you need to know about this family. I don't know why you're here, but it seems you've settled in nicely." He gives him a grin and then wiggles his eye brows. "She's become an attractive woman."

"It's not what you think. I ..."

"Listen, that's your business. She's just my sister." Damien puts his palms up towards Paul.

"It isn't ..."

"Whoa, I'm really not interested, so let it go." His voice is more determined this time around.

Paul shrugs his shoulders giving him the signal to go on.

"Ok, then. Let's get back to why I've come here. I thought I'd have some private time with you, but apparently not tonight, so we need to agree on a meeting. What are you doing tomorrow, say at noon, at *The Bubble Room* in Captiva? It's easy to find."

"Can you give me a hint of why you want to meet with me?"

"Actually, no, it's complicated. Just say that it is in your best interest to know what I know about this family. You'll have to trust me."

"This is all very strange."

"I take that as a yes. Tomorrow, noon, *The Bubble Room*. Just make sure you are not followed this time. Now, go back to your bed partner. I've got to shove this body through a tunnel. Oh, one more thing. Here are your credit cards that I took from you when I robbed that place. You're paying for lunch."

Damien leaves Paul alone in the bathroom. On his way to the closet he gives his sister one last glance. He is not sure how he feels about her. Maybe he'll figure that out one of these days, but not right now.

Paul climbs back into bed, not realizing Anne has overheard the two men's entire conversation. She knows what she must do.

The morning arrives without either one telling the other about what they know.

However, Julien is torn about sharing with Elizabeth anything about the secret meeting with Marcus.

Stranger on a Train

Julien busies himself most of the next day, yet is not able to put aside the life and death danger he believes Elizabeth is in. Further, he figures his own life would be in jeopardy if Marcus suspected that he told Elizabeth of the meeting. He's got to work out in his own mind the priorities. Nothing he concludes seems to settle the dilemma until he realizes he would rather be dead himself than be alive and without Elizabeth. Now he has only one thing he must do. He leaves his shop without having completed the car repair work that was started early this morning. That will have to wait. He has more important matters to deal with now.

A mile or so away from the Varro residence, he pulls his vehicle off the side of the road into a small clearing that is mostly hidden from traffic. He knows what he is about to do is final, and once completed, there is no way to reverse the action. He takes a deep breath and shuts off the engine. On the passenger side is a small box that contains a timing device that he intends to connect to the engine of Marcus's Porsche. Installed and properly set, the apparatus will ignite a fire once the sports car reaches a speed of 45 miles per hour. At that point the vehicle will be disabled and as a consequence of the fire be fatal to all passengers. He's worked this through his head enough times to believe there is no other way to save

Antonio Vianna

Elizabeth from her husband's wicked plan. It all depends on him. He will not let her down.

With as much conviction as he can marshal he takes the small box with a few tools, and heads for the Varro place. If done right, it will take him less than thirty minutes to get the job done. The walk to the house takes him longer, giving him time to reconsider idea, so he tries to think of something else. His own distraction works out well as he reaches his destination sooner than he had expected.

He quickly walks toward the garage where the Porsche is located. He mounts the timing device with great professional agility as would a surgeon using a scalpel, finishing in about twenty-five minutes. There are no interruptions. Making sure he does not leave any evidence at the scene, he scans the area as would a cheetah scouting for prey.

He is back to his vehicle sooner than expected. Now seated alone, he tosses the tools and empty box on the passenger side floor. He feels his heart start to race, accepting the condition as normal for what he's just done. He bows his head, giving himself the sign-of-the-cross, saying "Bless me father for I have sinned." He starts to cry.

A few more minutes pass with silence as his only companion. Julien starts the vehicle's engine and returns to his car repair shop to busy himself, promising not to begin second guessing himself along the way.

Stranger on a Train

Within the white house at 2763518 West Gulf Drive is a small room, full of canvases, brushes, paint, and other accessories used by Elizabeth. Painting in oil on canvas is more than a diversion for her; it is a calling that she takes quite seriously.

She's studied the works of various artists such as Henri Matisse, Wassily Kandinsky, Pablo Picasso, and Ernst Ludwig Kirchner, just to name a few. And while the oils by these diverse artists are different, to Elizabeth, they all are the same in that each tells a story.

For example, Picasso's *Seated Women* represents the image of a split personality that Freud previously proposed in his work dealing with three parts of one's personality. Picasso continued with this theme in much of his artistic endeavors including his writings when he used double meanings and visual puns.

Elizabeth knows she'll never be recognized as an artist by others, still she continues studying and painting just the same. Family members do not seem to share her interests, which to her to some degree, is well and good. Time alone doing what she loves is time well spent.

She dabs here and there on the canvas, smiling and talking to the visual objects in front of her, consumed by the passing time. She is unaware that someone is quietly looking in on her. She backs off a bit to take a look at what she's accomplished so far. Pleased with what she sees, she says, "Very nice," and then twirls her body around one time to continue the celebration.

Out of the corner of her eye she spots an uninvited caller. "Paul, what are you doing here?"

159

"I didn't mean to interrupt you, I'm sorry. I'll leave."

"Oh, no, please come. I rarely have anyone who comes here."

He sheepishly walks into the room. Immediately he recognizes it as belonging to an artist, much like the place where he writes. Untidy looking to others, but to the artist, everything has its place. He gives out a smile, feeling comfortable with the surroundings.

"Do you paint?"

"No. I understand my limitations."

"Have you ever tried painting?"

"No again."

"Then you really don't know your limitations if you haven't tested them, have you."

He tilts his head left to right a few times, "Maybe so, but I'd rather stick to writing. It's where I feel most comfortable."

She gives him a smile. "I understand the whole notion of feeling comfortable. That's why I'm here alone, by myself. I'm able to express myself without criticism from others."

"What happens when you have a showing? Does everyone compliment your work?"

"I don't show my work. They're for me, only me. I suppose that's one difference between us."

"Huh?"

"People read your books and have an opinion. They'll either buy another one of your books, or not. That doesn't happen with me."

"I see."

Stranger on a Train

"Perhaps and perhaps not," enjoying in a way the lack of specificity for the moment, but not for long.

"I don't understand. What do you mean?"

"At least you have the gumption. I lack the nerve to have others comment on my work. It's much safer that way. I think I'm thin skinned in some ways."

"But what if they actually like your paintings? Wouldn't you want to know that?"

"Compliments don't occur in a vacuum. They are accompanied some how and some way with an eventual criticism. I lack the courage to hear the bad comments."

"I have a hard time believing that. Without criticism you can't improve. It's not to say that you have to take all criticism seriously and do something with it. You can simply decide not to use the feedback. But if you don't get the feedback, you have no choice in the matter. Choices are good, don't you think?"

"Abstractly speaking, I agree. Personally speaking, I'm not so sure." She gives him a smile.

"To each his own … I guess. But if I don't get feedback I have no idea how good or bad my books are. It's only my opinion, not my readers' opinions."

"Our differences could be based on your interest in making money with your books. That's not the same with me. I'm not interested in making any money at all with my paintings. Money has a way of interfering with sound judgment."

"Why not donate the revenues from the sales of your paintings to a worthy cause? That way money is out of the picture."

"And my argument that about feedback is no longer valid?"

"In a way, yes."

"I wish it were that easy," returning to the lack of specificity where it is safer.

There is an automatic pause that seems programmed at this juncture in the conversation. They both remain silent for a short time.

"Would you sell me one of your paintings?"

The question takes Elizabeth by surprise. She frowns.

"I know you said you don't sell them, but you could consider this to be a private sale. No feedback in exchange, I promise."

She gives the proposition a consideration, and then comes up with one of her own. "No sale."

Paul's eyebrows curl in disappointment.

"But I'll consider a trade."

"A trade?"

"Yes. One of your books for one of my paintings."

His sulking face turns bright. "And we each select what the other will receive. You pick the painting and I pick the book."

"I think we've got a deal." She extends the free hand that is not holding the paintbrush towards Paul. They confirm the agreement with a hand shake.

They stare at one another a tad longer than normal. Elizabeth suspects something else is up, so she asks, "You have something to tell me, don't you. That's why you really came this way."

Paul's quick glance away is a sure sign of a cover up. They both know the truth, yet he is not willing to be part of the dance. He intends to do his best to play it down.

In a surprise move, she proposes something else, "You are fond of my daughter. Is that what you've come to tell me?"

While his initial intention was to tell her about Marcus's threat on her life, he is not prepared for what he hears. He does not recover fast enough to throw off the truth of Elizabeth's remark, yet he figures it is easier to handle his affection for Anne than her death threat. "I'm embarrassed."

She steps towards him and takes hold of his hand. "Don't be. She is a lovely young woman and is perfect for the right man." Her comments are with double meaning.

Paul thinks he's just stepped out of trouble, and has no inkling that he's in deeper turmoil than he could ever imagine. He feels compelled to say something. "Well, I am embarrassed, whether or not I should be. Please don't tell Marcus or Anne that I've mentioned this to you. I need to work out in my own mind how to approach Anne, and then, of course, your husband. I've got to do this just right. You understand."

Elizabeth gives him a motherly type smile, "Yes, this is just between the two of us."

He takes a deep sigh of relief that gives him a false sense of security. The sanctuary, however, will not last long as other forces emerge. Will he have enough strength to fend off the evil that awaits him?

In another part of the house, Marcus paces the floor, troubled over the predicament he is in.

On one hand, he thought he would be able to convince Paul that his help was essential in uncovering the murder of his son Damien. Further he believed he could sway the young man to believe that Anne was behind it all. Now he isn't so sure Paul is on his side. He has an itchy feeling that his daughter has gotten to him, and that Paul's allegiance is elsewhere.

On the other hand, he was assured that Julien would readily buy into the murder plot to get rid of his wife, especially when he held out the finances to buy him his own car repair shop. But, again, he miscalculated, and can't come up with a reasonable explanation for this. He wonders if there aren't invisible ghostly forces working against him.

Must he do everything himself? Can't he count on anyone for anything anymore? There was a time, he remembers, when you could rely on others to do things you didn't want to do yourself, but still had to be done. Everything and everyone had a price. Times have changed, so he thinks to himself, seeing no light at the end of the proverbial tunnel.

He takes comfort in reaching for the bottle of Dimple Scotch. This time, he pours a double shot into a tumbler. He swirls the dark alcohol around in the crystal glass to air out the liquid and then takes a full swallow. It runs down his throat, lubricating the passage to his pleasure. He smacks his lips in approval.

There is only one final person he might solicit for help. It's a long shot, he reckons, but without another option in the picture he decides to give it his best. He repeats the same swirl looking at the liquid changing color as it moves in a circular motion in the glass. In a way he is mesmerized by the physical transformation. Finally, he finishes off the rest of the scotch with one long mouthful.

He heads off to look for his daughter.

Within a few minutes Marcus is face to face with Anne. She seems to be in a hurry.

"I've going out for lunch with a friend."

"Anyone I know?" he innocently asks, trying to be friendly-like with his daughter.

She gives herself a secret smile, "No, I don't think so … just a few friends." She keeps up the fib suspecting he is up to something.

"I've something quite important to talk with you about."

"I see. Can it wait until I return? I should be back in a few hours. Then I'm all yours." She is polite and respectful. She knows the ways of her father.

"Well, I guess it will have to wait. I wouldn't want you to be late." He gives her a grin that can be interpreted as sincere or as sarcastic, most likely the latter. Both understand the intended version.

He lets her leave the house driving a yellow Mini Cooper, while he waits for only a few minutes before he follows her in his now rigged Porsche. He is careful to drive within the speed limit knowing how easy it is to be ticketed by the local police for all sorts of traffic violations. He doesn't want to be pulled over. Moreover, he can't afford being late. He has no idea that driving within the law today will literally save his life. He has no idea what to expect when he reaches the unknown destination, but instinctively is uneasy with it all.

Paul gets into the rented Impala, having decided to keep it for as long as he remains in Florida. He takes his time getting to the restaurant in Captiva. Traffic seems to be light at the moment.

Cleaned up and looking presentable Damien has already arrived at *The Bubble Room*. He waits next to a gift shop about fifty yards from the restaurant to look out for Paul. He does not expect any additional guests, yet he remains vigilant to keep under cover. It is nearly time, so he fidgets impatiently.

Across the street from the restaurant is a large parking area, unpaved. He keeps an eye out for cars entering the spot. Several vehicles come and go as he waits for someone special to walk towards the restaurant's front door. He begins to think the appointment is off, that Paul finked out. Disappointment begins to be a concern. He thinks that's his lot in life.

He shrugs his shoulders and decides to give it another fifteen minutes, and then he'll take off.

After Paul's Impala enters the parking area, a yellow Mini Cooper passes to enter a further away parking space just off the street. Then, after a few other cars pass by a Porsche swerves off to the left to end up in a spot at the far end of another street. These events go unnoticed by Damien since he has no awareness of who is driving what.

However, he sees Paul stop on the side of the street to look both ways before he crosses. Now about thirty feet away from Paul, Damien calls out. "Paul. Come here." He waves both hands calling him by his first name to make it more personal.

Paul looks up and for an instant does not recognize the man calling him. He gives off a frown, and then quickly makes him out. He lifts his head just so slightly and walks towards him. Soon the two men are face to face.

"This way," Damien says as he moves towards the gift shop.

Paul follows, yet not sure why.

Soon they are inside the small building that sells an assortment of souvenirs and trinkets mostly directed at the tourist crowd. A few people linger inside checking out tee-shirts, cups, and key rings. Damien moves to a place in the corner where there are no other people.

"From here we can see if anyone followed you. Let's just stay in here a while to make sure."

"Who do you suspect?"

"Everybody." Damien gives him a grin that both understand.

They look out the small window for a few seconds. Then Damien taps Paul on the shoulder. He motions with his head to look at someone walking across the street.

"Anne!" exclaims Paul.

Damien wiggles his eyebrows. "Let's wait a little more."

Both men stare through the window. Suddenly, Paul spots someone he knows. He gives Damien the same shoulder tap and head nod.

"My father." There is a little surprise in Damien's voice.

For a short time both men are quiet not sure what else there is to say. They think they've seen it all.

A few more minutes pass without much incidence. Paul asks, "What's next?"

"Just wait a few more minutes. Let's see what happens when my father and sister figure out you and your luncheon friend are not in the restaurant ..."

"And that your father was following Anne, unknown to her," Paul interrupts.

They give out a laugh that seems to act as some strange sort of bond between them. Is this the start of a relationship that will serve some future purpose?

Marcus and Anne finally end up in front of the restaurant. They seem to be arguing as best Paul and Damien can determine. Next to them is a large fake iron cage that children play in and tourists take pictures of, perhaps symbolic of the situation Marcus and Anne have found themselves in.

Damien says, "After they take off, let's get something to eat. I know of another place close by. It's sort of a dive, but the food's good and since you're buying, the price is right."

Paul answers, "Ok, lead the way, but you've got to tell me what is it that's so important."

Chapter 7

Driving alone Anne shakes her head, wondering how her father found out about the meeting, and further why Paul and her brother never showed up. Something fishy is going on that she is determined to find out.

She drives towards Ft. Myers. It should take her over an hour to get exactly where she is headed, *Santa's Bells and Whistles*, a twenty-four hour seven days a week adult entertainment spot. She is one of Santa's helpers, known as Misty.

As an exotic dancer, she is very good with moves that most other women only dream of doing, but that all men long for. She has a special way with men, usually remembering something about each of them to make them feel special. It goes beyond just their name; she has almost a photographic memory for names of people, something as a child she showed off with great pride. She'll often remind a man what they last talked about during the previous visit, which to the first timer is a shock. But, it seems to keep bringing them back again and again.

She earns most of her money through tips that are stuffed down her bra or inside her panties, when she is wearing them. Some men try to go beyond with a quick feel. She slaps their hands away successfully most of the time. Other money is simply thrown on the wooden dance floor that she picks up after each performance. Misty has made as much as five hundred dollars per night, usually a four hour shift. Not bad for tax free money.

After each performance, she usually gets into a skimpy outfit that barely fits her well endowed body, and then mingles with the crowd. While not charging anything to talk with anyone about anything that pleases them, even the weather or the price of a barrel of crude oil, she accepts an assortment of gifts in the form of money and jewelry. She turns down getaways and other kinds of trips. She's even rejected marriage proposals, although always welcomed the talk of settling down especially if a non-returnable engagement ring is offered in advance.

She actually loves what she does and she is good at it. Most important her skills are perceived valuable enough for her to get paid for them. What else could she hope for at this stage in her life?

There are three men who return on a regular basis to be with her, just to talk about all sorts of things. Each man comes during a different day of the week, never on the weekends. To her best estimation, they do not know one another, which for her is the optimal arrangement. First names are used.

Ted is a salesman, or at least that's what he claims to be. Good looking, about five years older than her, and a sharp dresser. In an odd way, she likes him the best, but can't figure out why, so she just lets the feeling last. He's given her an engagement ring that must have put him back several months of pay checks, but that's not her worry. She figures he's a big boy and knows what he is doing. While they haven't settled on an exact wedding date as yet, she knows that will never happen.

She'll try to string him along as much as possible and then give him some sort of story that will end it all.

They've had sex many times, something she enjoys immensely with him. He is quite imaginative and full of surprises.

She makes sure he wears protection to prevent her from becoming pregnant. She thinks he's single but these days you really can't tell for sure.

Alan is older than Ted, she figures about fifteen years as much. Balding in the middle of his head with a few threads of brown hair on the sides, he comes across to her more as a father figure. She likes talking with him because he is funny. He claims to own a family furniture store in Napes, about a fifty minute drive away. She doesn't really care where the place is, but it seems to matter to him.

They've never had sex, and she suspects that to be due to some sort of rule he lives by.

She suspects he is married with a few kids and the thought of having sex with someone other than his wife is not part of his moral guidelines. So be it, he makes her laugh and flowers her with gifts, mostly ornaments that are suitable as house furnishings. She thinks he's ripping off the accessories from the store's inventory.

Finally, there is Kyle. He's almost her same age and acts at times quite young, almost immature. She can't figure out how old he really is, but it would not surprise her to find out he is underage. Again, that's not her worry. She isn't the one who checks the IDs, that's someone else's job. He is very different than Ted and Alan in that she suspects Kyle to be gay or bisexual. She isn't sure, though.

They've never had sex and he's never brought up the topic, so she leaves the topic alone. He's told her that he works at a hospital in North Fort Myers as a physician's assistant.

She believes he is somehow affiliated with the medical field because he's thrown out medical terms to her at odd times during their conversation, but isn't exactly sure about his title or what he does. She remembers one such time when he told her how to kill someone using a Propofol injection. She recollects him saying that all it takes is a prick underneath the skin of a high dosage to render the person unconscious immediately, and then after painful involuntary muscle spasms, death eventually sets in.

Anne, aka Misty, thinks how each of these three men might help her in ways they never imagined. Could she somehow convince each of them of her endless love and devotion? Could she use her gift of persuasion and seduction to manipulate each of them in doing something they would otherwise not imagine doing? The more she thinks about it, the more credible it becomes. She gives herself a broad smile. She has the motive and now she thinks she just might have a means to her end. All she needs is the opportunity. She'll give it some more thought, although time is passing, so she can't wait forever.

"I'm amazed you're still sane after all you've been through," Paul says, still trying to come to grips with what Damien has told him of his still somewhat young life. The multiple failed attempts of suicide, along with being in and out of juvenile detention facilities would be too much for him to cope with. He shakes his head in somewhat disbelief. He's not that much older than the fellow sitting across the table, but their experiences are vastly different. It's strange how people turn out in life. Some make it through with ease as if they are on some sort of imaginary high tech roller skates smoothly gliding through life's ups and downs, and then there are those who don't seem to be able to put anything in their life together. They stumble and hit every pot hole in life as if that was their true destiny.

"Don't get the impression that I'm just fine with my life. I've got lots of problems to work out; some of which may never see the light of day. Hey, I stole from that convenience store and took your wallet. Is that an example of having it together?" Damien gives Paul a grin, the kind that says "not on your life."

The two men continue to look at each other, not real sure what to make of it. It is strange that they should be together having lunch as if they were old school friends just

Antonio Vianna

trying to catch up on the news with each other. They seem
to hit it off quite well in spite of their dissimilarities. Imagine
one modification in their life here and another change there
might have resulted in them being totally different today, even
perhaps the exactly like the other person. It's scary in a way
that there are a few seminal events in each of our lives that
shape who we become.

"You're not alone," Paul says. Yet while the words seem to
carry little weight since his life's problems have not nearly been
as critical as those faced by Damien, he has no idea the hidden
dangers up ahead. Is it prophetic or just a polite phrase to keep
their conversation going?

"We're all alone. Don't bet on counting on anyone to help
you out unless there is something in it for them." Damien's
face is now quite serious, the words emphasizing the disparity
between their separate outlooks on life.

"So, what's in it for you?"

Damien frowns, "For me?"

"Yeah, for you. You returned my wallet, driver's license
and credit cards. You've told me about your dysfunctional
family who don't seem to like each other. What do you want
in return?" He pauses and then finishes the rest of the thought.
"By the way I haven't forgotten that you've kept the cash." He
gives Damien a smirk.

"Maybe this is one of these times when there is a free gift."
His face mirrors that of Paul.

"Oh yeah." Paul rolls his eyes. "Just give it to me. I'm ready
to hear you out."

Stranger on a Train

Damien fiddles with the remaining cold fries on his plate. He feels a little gas moving its way through his body and he wonders if he can shut it down. He can't so he lets out a fart.

Paul laughs, "well that says it all."

Damien joins in with a chuckle of his own. "Now that I've cleared my throat, let me continue."

Paul waits.

"I want to get even with my father for everything he's done to me. I told you about my young sister, Edna, how he killed her."

Paul interrupts, "You said it was accidental, didn't you?"

"Doesn't matter. He made a life of hell for her, for me, for Anne, and definitely for my mother. I'm surprised Anne or my mother haven't found a way to do him in." He looks off to no place in particular. "They're probably just too afraid to get rid of him." He turns his face back to Paul, "I wouldn't mind doing it myself."

"You wouldn't kill him, would you?"

"Sometimes, when I was alone in juvenile, I'd think of all kinds of ways to kill him. I came up with some pretty bad ways, believe me on this." He takes a sip of water from a glass nearby to quench his dry mouth. He nods his head, indicating how real the remembrances are to him right now. His body quivers ever so slightly. "If I don't watch it I can get real angry and lose it. Yeah. Real angry." His voice trails off.

Paul feels a shiver take over his body just looking at Damien tell his story. He grabs for the water glass in front of him, with ice cubes essentially left. He moves the glass in a way that spins the pieces of frozen water around, and then at the right time, tosses one small cube into his mouth. He starts nervously chewing it all the time scrutinizing the man seated in front of him who appears icy cold to him, cut off from reality as an ice berg floating away unattached from a glacier. He wonders if the purpose of this meeting is for Damien to get him to help kill his father, or worse for him to do it himself.

Damien offers some relief, "Don't worry, I'm on my meds."

However, the words conjure up another worry in Paul's mind. He feels the pressure mount. He starts chewing on another piece of ice. Then he manages to say, "Just don't do anything foolish." Once the advice leaves his lips he wonders its usefulness, but it's too late, the words are out.

Damien seems to ignore the counsel either because he doesn't hear it, too preoccupied with his own thoughts, or else, he's heard the suggestion many times before that now it leaves less of an imprint. He shifts to something else. "As I said to you earlier, when I figured out that you were staying at the house, I had to find out why you were there. They usually don't have many visitors. And now that I know you were hired to tutor Anne … that's a crock … I'm convinced my father has something up his sleeve that somehow includes you. I'd be careful around him." It seems from his now twisted face he has something more to say. However, he doesn't let on to Paul. He remains quiet.

Paul is not willing to tell him what he knows or believes he knows about the goings on in the house. He's just not ready to trust Damien, so he too keeps quiet for a little while longer.

"Now my sister, well she is something else." He rolls his eyes. "I've seen how you too have gotten to know each other. I bet she's tutoring you on things she knows more about than you." He grins.

"It's not what you think."

"Oh, then what is it?"

Paul has no ready answer. He has nothing to back it up, so he keeps silent.

"Anyway, that doesn't matter to me. You'll deal with her your own way, I'm sure of it."

Paul is not sure now what else there is to talk about, yet he thinks there is more to learn from Damien. He doesn't know how to approach him. He waits for a bomb to explode right before him, but it doesn't.

"That's all I got, my friend. I'm headed back to my sea castle where I'll contemplate my life, drink some beer, and without a doubt steal a few more odds and ends to keep up my life style." He moves his tongue around inside his mouth, a nervous habit that Paul notices for the first time.

"So, uh, we won't be seeing each other again?"

"Well, that's one of the sadness's of life. Don't call me, I'll call you." Damien stands and extends a hand for a goodbye shake. He leaves Paul alone.

As Damien walks away, Paul has the urge to shout out to him, to bring him back for more talk, but doesn't. He isn't sure why. He wonders if there was some sort of hidden message that he missed during the conversation, yet he can't come up with anything. He knows he's not a hero, and for sure, has no intention to becoming one. Yet, has some force of fate brought him to the Varro residence at this point in time to make him one. He hopes not.

Damien, on the other hand has different ideas.

Like in the story of Dr. Jekyll and Mr. Hyde, where Jekyll is the caring doctor and Hyde is his wicked side, Damien is also haunted by an internal conflict within his personality.

The primitive side of his personality, where his urges, desires and aggressive impulses come from, is at times mostly unconscious to him. He is really not aware of their existence until they suddenly erupt. Damien has immediate hungers, albeit hidden deep within his psyche most of the time. They are driven by wanting total gratification. Further, he does not consider the personal costs in seeking this goal nor the impact it might have on others. This is the Mr. Hyde part of his personality. Some might consider this to be unrestrained expression while others call it evil.

Most of the time there are few opportunities for instant satisfaction, however, those people who seek this on-the-spot pleasure find themselves in serious trouble. Damien is one such person. While restraining his urges is partially voluntary, some of these actions are outside his consciousness. It is the unconscious internal struggle he faces every day.

He's not all bad, however. There is a good side to him that when exposed makes him appear to be a good person, the kind of person you'd like to have lunch with or simply chat with.

Stranger on a Train

Perhaps this is the kind of person who you would even trust. It is this part of his personality that seeks to control his wants of immediate satisfaction from all sorts of things. This is when he gratifies his whims, itches, fancies, and the like, but only when it is morally right to do so, not simply when he can get away with it or when he thinks it is simply practical. He has learned some good things from experience, parents, and teachers when he was a young boy, but not nearly enough.

Unfortunate for him, there was not much in this area to learn positive lessons. His earlier life was full of temptations and experiences that were visible and repetitive. He learned just the wrong things from just the wrong people, and today, he is not a good person.

He is not like Dr. Jekyll, but more like Mr. Hyde.

Could he have been cast to become this type of person with little opportunity to be something different? Are his parents to blame for how he's turned out, with some help from his sister, or could he have overcome those obstacles? In other words, did he really have any choice in the matter? Further, can he change even if he wants to?

The fact of the matter is Damien has no intention of changing who he is. He figures that's the way the dice rolled and he intends to live it out for as long as he is around on the planet. His cardinal intention is to get even with his father, and for the moment, that's all he is focused on. He figures Paul can be of some help in implementing his plan if he can just get him hooked. All he needs to do is make Paul believe they have similar if not identical goals. He starts some serious thinking about this as he continues walking.

Antonio Vianna

By the time he climbs down the metal stairs of the barge he's got most of the plan figured out. He's happy with what he's come up with, and the more thought he gives to it the more convinced it will work. He pops open a can of beer and starts slurping down its contents. Now, he only needs to pin point the exact time to put the plan into motion. After a few more beers he falls asleep.

Elsewhere, Anne is scheming something up herself.

There is a light crowd at *Santa's Bells and Whistles*, not unusual for the time of day. Misty is readying herself for the first performance of her shift. She peeks out from behind a curtain to see if she recognizes anyone, and once she spots a man in the first row she smiles.

There is a short pause in the music to separate the last dancer's performance from hers. Once the previous dancer, Flame, leaves the stage, Misty gets ready for her entrance. Spot lights are turned down for a few seconds and then the brightness is increased. A well known song starts, and for those in the audience who recognize it know that Misty is about to appear. Hoots and hollers call out from the crowd. The sounds stir her up.

Once her scantily dressed body is fully encased in the spot light, she begins her performance. It lasts twenty minutes, much too short for the wild audience, and too long for her.

Stranger on a Train

She'll be repeating the same moves three more times within the next four hours, so she needs to keep up her energy. Additionally, she's got to have enough liveliness when she works on individual patrons. One such person especially comes to mind now. She can't wait to do her mo – jo.

After the last move ends, she disappears behind the curtain, yet the crowd continues screaming for an encore. "More – more – more," they yell. She loves the attention and feels all tingly. She prepares to work the crowd.

With just a see-through shawl but nothing else to cover her breasts, the same spiked heals, and a skimpy bikini to barely hide her crotch, she begins to roam through the crowd. She takes a seat next to a man who seems to be intoxicated. On top of the small cocktail table is a pile of bills. She gives him of her best smiles, "How'd you like my performance?"

He grabs a five dollar bill to slide over to her side of the table, too drunk to give her a quick feel like most men do when they stuff it between the bikini strap and her smooth skin.

She's thankful for his inebriation. She moves on quickly concluding there is nothing more coming.

Sitting at the next table are two younger looking men she figures to be military personnel on leave, probably just finished with boot camp. Their hair is closely cropped and their posture is erect. She thinks this might be their first time at a strip club. She sits down on an empty chair and decides to keep her legs apart for them to get a good look. It's the least she can do for her country, she tells herself. They seem to be fit and full of vigor, and she starts to wonder how it would be to be with the two of them at the same. It wouldn't be the first time for her.

She wiggles her eyebrows to increase the tease as she leans over to let her breasts press against the shawl. The two men remain quiet, just looking in awe what is right before them.

"How'd I do?" That's really all she needs to say since few people actually listen to her words. They're usually too focused on what they see, not what they hear, which is just fine with her.

Each man grabs their beer bottle for a gulp, lost for words at the moment, yet eyes that were once glued to her crotch now refocus to her breasts. They remain quiet.

She waits only a few seconds and then shoves off realizing they don't get it. "Maybe another time," she whispers just loud enough in a sexy voice for them to hear.

Watching her all the time is Kyle, the physician's assistant who knows something about Propofol.

She knows he's been looking at her, probably getting jealous every time she sat down to talk with someone other than him. She savors those thoughts believing them to be true. She walks towards him. "May I sit down?" she asks in a seductive and innocent like way.

He picks up on the game, "As long as you mean me no harm."

She frowns to herself thinking how strange his answer is, yet takes her place along side him. "How have you been … work and all?" It's as if two good friends are about to chit chat over a cup of coffee.

"You know … the same old stuff. Some patients live and some die." He seems apathetic about it all.

She senses something else is up. He's usually livelier when they talk. "What's up? You don't sound right."

"Trouble's brewing over the pass." He takes a sip of beer not showing any emotion at this point.

She decides to continue with another question, "What kind of trouble?"

It seems that's all it takes for him to open up to her. "The hospital is about to layoff a bunch of people. I think I'm one of them."

An empathetic look appears on her face, "I'm sorry to hear about that, but I'm sure you can find another job quickly."

"I'm not sure of that. Not many hospitals are hiring these days. I don't want to relocate. I like it here."

Timing is everything. "Do you have enough money to hold you over until you find something?"

He gives her a disappointed frown, "No." The one word says it all.

"Maybe I can help."

"I'm not going to take money from you. I'm not looking for a handout." He puckers his lips, firm in his conviction.

"Who said anything about giving you anything? I might know how you can make some good money using your medical know how."

He leans over. "Go on."

"Listen, I really can't talk more about this here, right now. I've got to circulate. But, later on, when my shift is over with, let's meet and I'll tell you what I'm thinking about."

"Sounds like a plan. I'll meet you outside when you're done here."

She gives him a reassuring smile and leaves him alone. He wonders what she is up to.

Later that same day Misty and Kyle meet outside the club. "Follow me," she says to him as she gets into her car, now dressed in conservative casual clothes, unrecognizable as a stripper.

She gets on Interstate 75 to head towards the Southwest Florida International Airport, taking Exit 131. She drives carefully thinking along the way the exact words to use to get him committed to do away with Paul and Damien.

While she isn't completely sure what Paul and Damien are up to, she mistakenly believes they don't know she's on to them. A miscalculation could cost her in the end. For the moment, she's got to make Kyle believe she has enough money to pay him for the deeds. She's convinced she can do this. The only other problem might be his conscience. Can she persuade him otherwise? She is going to give it her best shot.

He follows the yellow Mini Cooper, also deep in is own thoughts. He wonders exactly what she is up to and why they are driving towards the Airport to meet. Not able to arrive at any opinion, he tells himself to keep an open mind. Opportunities come up when you least expect them, but you just have to be careful of what may seem to be too good to be true, because, it might not be true at all. While self-confidence might interfere with sound judgment, he reasons he is too smart to let that happen to him.

Finally, they park their vehicles next to each other. She motions to him to get out of his car to join her. He sits quietly in the passenger seat of the Mini Cooper. She is the first to speak.

"I love airports. They make me feel free and independent." She looks directly ahead, through the bug filled front window as if she is alone, by herself, just talking aloud some thoughts. Then she turns to him. "Do you like airports?"

He is not sure how to answer it so he shrugs his shoulders, "Yeah, I guess so." He twists his face, mostly with his lips to one side, not following her completely, at least not yet.

She just looks at him without much emotion for a few seconds as if she is contemplating whether to go on or not. However, she's already decided on him as the mark, her accomplice, so she goes on. "There is one man in my life harassing me, and I can't stop him, at least not alone. I need your help."

Kyle shifts his body in the leather seat not quite sure where this is all headed. "Go on. I'm listening." He's not sure whether she's believable right now.

"My brother, he's the one."

He wonders what she is considering. "What about him?"

She starts to cry real tears, although the emotion is all an act. In between the sobbing she manages to say, "He's raped me, over and over again. I can't go on." She leans his way just enough to make it easy for him to hold her in his arms. It works.

He shifts his body closer to hers and grabs onto her, tightly to him. He doesn't have the words to console her right now, but that's not what she is looking for.

She begins to reel him in. "I can't tell my mother. She wouldn't believe me. I can't go to the police. They'd say I probably had it coming, you know, with what I do at the club. You're the only one I can think of." She takes hold of him, faking the quiver in her words.

"What do you want me to do?" He's not yet feeling the full effect, and she senses it as well.

She realizes that the first try was too weak of an argument, so she decides to step it up. She pulls ever so slightly away from his hold to look him squarely in the eyes. Watery spots still cling to her face. "I want him to go away forever. I never want to see him again." She keeps looking at him for signals. She knows that she's got his attention, the first stage of the persuasion process. That's clear. But she now wonders if he understands what she is really saying. It appears not fully.

"I'm not following you. How can I get him to disappear?"

"Kyle, I need you to kill him, somehow, maybe using a drug or something. I don't know how, I just know it's got to be done before I go insane. That's the only sure way he'll be gone from my life once and for all. I can pay you whatever you think is reasonable." She believes she's made it as clear as possible but she's got to be sure there is enough emotion in the delivery. She starts to cry again. "I need you."

"You're kidding me!" He can't believe what he's just heard.

In between the sobs, she tells him, "No I'm not. You need the money and I have money to give you." She pauses for a moment to accentuate the next part, "But you need to do something for me in return. It's all very simple."

The moment of truth for any persuasion is that critical point at which the other person agrees with what you are saying to accept the soundness and importance of the message. This point can be at any moment, but it can also be reversed as quickly as it is originally accepted. She waits to find out what he does next.

"I've never done this before. I'm not sure I can do it."

She's goes on her instincts that now all she has to do is sweet talk him, to calm down his apprehensions and give him reassurance. "I believe in you. I know you want to relieve me of my pain. I know this as much as I know my name. We can plan this out together so that it is fool proof. How much do you need? I can give you, say, a few thousand dollars now, and another five thousand dollars when it's done." While this might not be much money to kill one person, Kyle is not a professional assassin nor has she ever paid someone to murder. Both accomplices are wading their way through the murky water. She lets the words linger above him to settle in. She squeezes his arm, "Please, I beg of you. Help me." She rests her head on his shoulder and waits for his deliberation.

Kyle takes a deep breath, taking in air and letting it out. He feels a little dizzy right now and his stomach seems to be working overtime. Acid starts to creep up his esophagus so he takes a deep swallow. The silence is agonizing to her, but goes unnoticed by him.

She wonders if this is a good time to slip her hand in between his legs to further encourage him to see it her way. She is about to make her move when he gives his answer.

"Ok, I'll do it." As dreadful of a response this might seem to many, it is said without much emotion from him, and it is pleasing to her ears.

"Oh, thank you so much. Thank you." Real tears form in the corners of her eyes that she intends to show off to him. She reaches for his face so that they stare at each other as if to seal the deal. She lets him look at her long enough to minimize the chance he'll back out. She's got more to say, having prepared part of the plan in advance. "I really don't know where my brother lives …." She is interrupted.

"What's his name? Do I need to know his name?" Kyle isn't sure what he should say, so he lets out whatever comes to his mind. He's still shaken from the agreement. His voice quivers enough that lets on his nervousness.

"You don't need to know his name. Just forget about that part. It's going to be alright. I know you can do this for me." She kisses him lightly on his lips to help him settle down. It seems to work, so she continues. "Like I said, I don't know where he lives … I'm pretty sure it's close by. I'll find that out." She's already got a way to locate his living place, assuming Paul goes along with another plan she's already prepared.

"When is this all going to take place? I mean when do I do it? I need some time to think about how I'm going to make this happen. You know …."

"Yes I know you do." She gives him a supportive smile. Her voice is soft and reassuring as if she is sending her child off

188

to school on the first day. "Let's meet in two days at the club. I'll have all the information you need by then." She reaches again for his face and plants a big kiss on his lips with a little tongue added for good measure. Once she figures he's been satisfied to her liking she pulls away. "Ok, I've got to go, and so do you. When we meet I'll have some money for you." She stares at him in a way that says he needs to leave her car now and get a move on.

He picks up on the signal and soon they separately drive off, he with his head still swirling about whereas she is calm, cool, and collected.

She heads to make contact with Paul, and has just the right story to tell him.

"I've got something important to tell you. I think you'll find it interesting."

Paul stops reading *Bound and Determined*, a mystery novel by one of his favorite contemporary authors. He looks up but says nothing.

She takes a nearby chair. "I know you've been talking with my brother, Damien." She lets the message sink it. It's an important point with significant implications so she doesn't want to rush it.

A swoosh of air swirls into his opened mouth, but nothing comes out.

"I thought you'd be surprised."

He regains some of his lost composure, but not all. "How do you know that?" Should he let on that he saw her and Marcus snoop around outside *The Bubble Room* or should he keep that between Damien and him? He decides to wait a little to see what she says.

"Let's just say a little birdie told me." She gives him a cute-like smile.

"You're not telling me everything."

"Either are you."

"What if I've met him? So what? I thought you said he was dead. Isn't that what you told me?" He thinks he's got the upper hand and feels good about it, but he's not even close to being even with the cunning woman seated next to him. He should be more careful.

"Let me remind you that all I said was Damien disappeared shortly after we moved into this house. Further, I said at that time we didn't know where he might be, or if he was alive or dead." She hesitates. "You might remember that I had a little conversation with you soon after you arrived. I asked you not to tell my father about it. You remember, don't you?" She pauses a second time before continuing. "You must have heard from my father that Damien was dead, not from me or anyone else because that's what he believes. In fact, he believes that Damien was murdered. Isn't that right?" Now she waits for Paul to respond. She knows she's got him cornered and savors the feeling.

He thinks about what she's said; now knowing he's jumped the gun. The silence continues until she breaks in.

"I hope I've been helpful in you remembering all of this."
She gives him another one of her cute-like smiles, except this
time there is a lot of sarcasm mixed in.

"Ok, I now remember. Let's call a truce."

"I didn't know we were fighting, but just the same, Ok,
it's a truce."

"So why are you letting me know you're aware that Damien
and I have talked?"

She gives him a surprised look. "He's my brother and he's
been gone from this house for a long time. Don't you think
I'd like to see him, find out what he's been up to? Come on,
he's my brother." The concerned sister role she plays out is
convincing.

Paul shrugs his shoulders. "He doesn't have much positive
things to say about the family. I'm surprised you'd want to see
him again."

"That's between him and me, not you. It's a family
matter."

"I stand corrected … my apology. So what do you want
from me? I suspect there is something."

"Yes, and I'm glad you asked. I want to meet him … alone
… just the two of us. I've got a lot to tell him. It'll be cathartic
for me, and it might be the same for him. I don't want my
father or mother to know about it, no one other than Damien,
you and me. Can you arrange a private meeting between him
and me soon? I'd very much appreciate it."

The request seems reasonable to him … a sister wanting
to make amends with her brother. However, he wonders if
Damien is up to it. He just didn't seem like the kind of person

who would want to do it, but he isn't sure. "I think that's awful loving of you to want to meet him, but I don't know if he feels the same."

"Could you ask him? If that's the best you can do, then just ask him."

"Of course." Paul is the one who hesitates for a split second. "But, I don't know where he lives. He's contacted me in the past, not the other way around. I'm going to have to wait for him get in touch with me." He curls his forehead. "Sorry."

"Well, that's how it is … nothing either one of us can do anything about that. Will you let me know when you've talked with him? It would mean a lot to me." She seems sincere, but it is for a sinister reason.

She now has to make sure Kyle doesn't back out. The arrangement may take a little longer to make happen than she anticipated.

A day later, Marcus and Elizabeth argue over money. It's a real free for all.

"I need more money. That's simple enough to understand." His face is red from all the shouting. It's his third Scotch within the last forty-five minutes.

"Yes it is simple to understand, and that's why it's a no answer. You're spending my money as if I am printing it in a back room. Further, you are not responsible with it. You spend it on all sorts of worthless things."

"Who says they're worthless?"

"I do and it's my money." Her voice is scratchy sounding, not accustomed to all the screaming and yelling. She feels her heart start to race, so she tells herself to settle down.

He glares at her in a menacing way, and then swallows the remains of alcohol from the crystal tumbler.

"Stay away from the booze. It'll kill you before your time."

He turns to her fighting mad. "Don't tell me what to do. I'll do whatever I want to do." He reaches to pour another double shot of Scotch. Part of the alcohol dribbles on the floor; his hands now a little unsteady. "Get out of my sight." He turns his back to her.

Elizabeth, now visibly upset, feels she needs to physically leave him right now, perhaps for good as often implied from Julien. Her lover has told her over and over again that she's too good to be with a man like him. Maybe now is the time to act on that message. Without uttering a word she walks away from Marcus. As she passes a glass platter she notices the keys to the Porsche. Without thinking much about it, she grabs them to head for the garage.

Moments later, Marcus hears the engine of the Porsche rev up. Confused at first, he stays put. The crystal tumbler is still firmly clenched in his hand. He turns around towards where Elizabeth previously stood to realize he is alone. Nothing makes sense for the next few seconds, his brain too frazzled from the effects of the alcohol.

Antonio Vianna

The car engine's sound quickly fades away as Elizabeth drives off to be with Julien. She feels exhilarated with a sense of freedom, intending to tell Julien how much she loves him and is now prepared to divorce Marcus. She presses on the accelerator pedal to cut down the driving time as much as possible. She shifts into fourth gear and steps on the pedal even more. Before shifting into the fifth gear the Porsche reaches 45 miles per hour. She does not make it to be with her lover. The timing device Julien secretly installed in the car to kill Marcus functions properly as Elizabeth reaches the threshold speed of 45 miles per hour. The car bursts into flames and rolls over several times. She is killed immediately.

Now asleep on the couch from too much drinking, Marcus snores, unaware of his wife's fatality. The bottle of DIMPLE Scotch is opened and half empty. One crystal tumbler rests on the floor nearby his sleeping body. At first, he does not hear the Sanibel Police officer knock on the door to give him the news of his wife's condition.

The police officer, however, is persistent. "Mr. Varro. This is the Sanibel Police. Please open. It is important." He pounds louder on the wooden door.

Still, Marcus continues in the booze driven slumber, not awakened by the sounds.

Stranger on a Train

The police officer is about to leave when Paul pulls up. The officer looks Paul's way as he approaches the door. "What's going on?"

"Who are you? Are you a family member?"

"No, I'm here for a short time to tutor Anne Varro. What's the matter?"

Uninterested in answering Paul's question, the police officer says, "I'm here to speak with Mr. Varro."

"Oh, I see." He shrugs his shoulders. "Well, come on in. I'll see if he's here. Sometimes he sits in the back yard." Paul unlocks the door and walks in, followed by the police officer.

"Have a seat and I'll check it out." Paul proceeds towards the back yard but stops before he gets half way. He spots Marcus sprawled out on the couch. He takes in a whiff of air and smells alcohol. He stops wondering what to do next, but doesn't have to wait long to make a decision.

The police officer is right behind him. "He's passed out. Go make some coffee while I bring him to." He reaches for a stick of smelling salt to restore Marcus's wakefulness.

Paul obeys the police officer's order, and within a few more minutes returns with a pot of coffee and three cups. Marcus, by this time, is slowly feeling the effects of the ammonium carbonate stimulant.

The three men drink the black beverage in silence until the police officer speaks. "Mr. Varro, I'm sorry to tell you this, but your wife has been in a car accident."

At first, the news is slow to sink in, yet Paul gets the drift of the message quickly. "How is she?"

The police officer ignores him, still looking at Marcus. "Do you understand what I'm saying, Mr. Varro. Your wife has been in a car accident."

While Paul is not pleased with being snubbed, he understands the reason, so he waits for Marcus to say something. It is slow in coming.

Marcus smacks his lips and takes another long sip of the black coffee. "Yes, I hear you. How is she?" The words are without much emotion, sort of distant and cold like.

The detached response does not go unnoticed by the police officer. "You don't seem much concerned. Is there a reason for that, or am I just misinterpreting it?"

"To be honest, we had a fight and she took off. I continued drinking my favorite beverage and passed out. Right now I'm not much in the mood to carry on a dialogue. Does that help explain it?" His demeanor continues to be remote but now there is an added unfriendliness that is mixed in. His head begins to ache so he starts rubbing his forehead.

The police officer is not sure he should tell Marcus the entire truth under these conditions. He hesitates, but in the end decides to fully disclose. "The accident was fatal. I'm sorry, but your wife did not make it."

While the full impact of the report would be shocking to most people, as it is to Paul, its effect does not seem to bother Marcus. Is the reason because he is not thinking clearly enough, or is there something else?

"My God," Paul says. "She's dead?"

The police office nods his head, finally recognizing a comment from Paul.

Stranger on a Train

"Marcus, I'm very sorry." Then Paul turns to the police officer, "When can we see her."

"I don't think you want to view the body. It's pretty much burned beyond recognition." The police officer's eyes are saddened, yet relieved that he's done with telling them of her death. He's always dreaded this part of his job.

Suddenly, Marcus seems alert, but just for a short time, recognizing what's been going on around him. "Dead, Elizabeth is dead." His voice is subdued. While it may appear he is grieving the loss, he is thinking about her will and how long it will take to finalize his inheritance.

"I'm sure you will notify other members of the family," the police officer says, looking at Marcus who is quiet.

"There's Anne. She'll be devastated," Paul says, his voice high pitched.

"Is she a daughter?"

"Yes," answers Paul all the while Marcus remains silent.

"Where is she now?"

Paul looks at Marcus for an answer. "Marcus, do you know where Anne is?"

"No. I have no idea." The response is short and without much feeling.

The police officer finds the entire discussion disturbing, sensing all along there is something else going on that is not currently transparent to him. He wonders if any of that is relevant, or if it is just weird.

Marcus doesn't seem sorrowful at all, at least not his external appearance. Has he just not come to grips with the reality of his wife's death, or doesn't he care one way or another?

Antonio Vianna

During previous experiences when the police officer has had to tell family members of catastrophic news there's always been emotional outbursts of some kind. Not this time, not with the deceased woman's husband. He figures he'll have more to go on once the root cause of the accident is revealed and if the woman's autopsy uncovers anything suspicious.

He decides he's done with these two men for now, so he stands up to leave. "Mr. Varro, I'm again sorry for your loss. We're going to take a close look at the vehicle, although I must say there isn't much left to look at, to determine why the car went off the road and burst into flames. Secondly, in these types of fatalities, we customarily perform an autopsy of the body. Unless you object, we'll do that and let you know what we find, if anything of relevance. I think that should do it for now. Let me know if I can do anything else. I can find my way out." He walks away.

Paul has the last word, "Nice meeting you. Thanks."

While the police officer hears his words, he also picks up the sarcasm spread on them, like peanut butter on bread, loud and clear.

Paul turns to Marcus wondering what kind of emotional support he can offer the man. Nothing comes to mind, so he asks. "Marcus, I'm very sorry about all of this. Whatever I can do, just let me know." He expects some sort of response but gets nothing. He wonders along the same lines as the police officer if something is up.

As if he is alone without anyone to talk or listen to Marcus stands and looks around the room for something. He turns his body, almost in a pivoting motion until he spots what he is looking for.

All the while Paul looks at him confused, wondering what it is all about. He decides to keep quiet, just keep watching.

Marcus moves towards the empty crystal tumbler on the floor, bends over, and picks it up. He walks towards the open bottle of DIMPLE Scotch to pour a shot. He makes a circular motion with the glass, still focused on its contents, and then takes a full gulp, empting the container in one swallow. While quiet throughout the entire activity, Marcus tosses through his mind the estimated value of his inheritance. He doesn't give it a bit of consideration that he may not be in Elizabeth's will at all, but if he is to inherit something, it might not be much. A grin appears on his face, showing for the first time in a while an emotional expression.

Then, for some reason, he senses he is not alone. The facial expression disappears as he turns to catch sight of Paul. "How long have you been here? I didn't hear you come in."

Paul is not sure how to respond, but regardless, Marcus has more to say. In a monotone voice he continues, "Elizabeth is dead … killed somehow in a car accident. I've got to tell Anne. She'll be sad. Those two were close." He pours another drink and walks to sit in a chair.

Paul continues to look on, now feeling very uneasy about all of it. He considers that Marcus is in some sort of trance, in a way traumatized by the tragic news. But, can he help the man? He has no experience in these matters and his instincts are not kicking in.

Antonio Vianna

"I need just a little rest. You'll excuse me, won't you?" Marcus closes his eyes as the glass slips out of his hand, spilling the scotch on the carpet floor. The glass hits the floor with a dull thud. Soon Marcus is asleep.

Paul decides to take an empty chair and wait for Marcus to awake or for Anne to arrive. A few hours pass, all along Paul's nerves are on edge.

It is now close to ten in the evening. Marcus continues to sleep and Anne has not come home. Paul decides he just might go to his bedroom and get as much sleep himself before tomorrow, which he suspects will be a hectic day. He falls asleep although with some difficulty within an hour. He tosses and turns in bed.

Sometime after midnight, Damien makes his way to visit Paul who is asleep. He uses the secret tunnel. He needs money, and rather than risk his life robbing another store, he hopes to find some sympathy. He has no idea what else to expect from the unexpected visit. He soon finds out.

He walks to the bed where he sees Paul shifting his body, a sure sign of being tensed. He shakes Paul on the shoulder a few times until he wakes up. The two men stare at each for a split second until Paul says, "What are you doing here?"

Without any hesitation Damien says, "I need a few bucks. I thought you'd help me out."

200

Paul sits up in bed, now rubbing his eyes. "What? You want me to give you some money?"

"Yes."

"Why?"

"Because I asked for it, and you feel sorry for me."

"I don't believe this."

"Doesn't matter what you believe. Just give me fifty dollars. I'm good for it."

"Right." Paul gives out a disapproving chuckle.

"You don't think I'll pay you back?"

"Again, right."

Damien stares ahead hoping the silence is sufficient to break down Paul. However, he is surprised at what comes next.

Without thinking about what to say next, Paul blurts out, "Your mother died in a car accident. I'm sorry."

At first it doesn't register with Damien as he continues to look at Paul in silence. Then, there is a connection. "My father did it." His eyes bulge.

"No, I don't think so."

"Don't tell me. I know him. I know what he's capable of doing. I'm going to get him if it is the last thing I do." With each passing word, his anger increases. His head starts to involuntarily bobble as if the movement and words are somehow interconnected.

"She died in a car accident. Your father was passed out, drunk, when the Sanibel Police and I arrived here. He had no idea."

Damien does not want to hear any of it. He's too convinced of his own conclusion. "If he didn't actually do it, he had someone else do it. He's ultimately responsible."

Paul begins to feel a little weird talking with Damien from his bed, so he gets up. Now faced to face with each other Paul says, "And I've got something else to tell you. Want to hear it?"

Damien does not want to get off the subject, too stirred up to think about anything else. Yet Paul is persistent.

"Your sister wants to meet you, one on one. Just name the time and place. I'll let her know. I think it's a good idea." He looks at Damien to see if any of this makes sense. He knows he's dumped a lot of family matters on him all at once, but it's done. There is nothing he can do about it now. In a way he's relieved it's all out there with nothing else to hold back.

Damien blinks his eyes a few times as if to clear his mind. It takes a few more tries to get him to answer. "Ok, if she wants that. Did she say why?"

"I think she just wants to connect with you. It's been a while since you saw each other, hasn't it?"

Damien doesn't answer. He is already thinking about how to use his sister to get back at his father. He knows she's as devious as him, so he has to be careful with her. He doesn't want to get the short end of the stick; better her than him if it comes down to it.

Paul recognizes when someone is thinking about one thing as you are talking about something else. That's exactly what Damien is about right now, so he waits a little before saying anything more. The delay is short. "I'll let her know. What time and what place are best for you?"

Damien pops out of his inner thoughts as his head lifts slightly towards Paul. "Uh, any time and any place. I'm pretty flexible as long as it's on the islands. I don't have wheels to cross over the Causeway."

"Do you have a driver's license? I could loan you my rental."

Damien gives him a twisted look that tells his answer.

"Yeah, I guess not."

Damien agrees with a slight nod of his head. Then he adds something that changes the meeting with Anne, "Right before getting on the Causeway as you leave Sanibel, to the right, is a public beach access area. There's a small parking lot and a boat ramp there. Have her meet me tomorrow at midnight. She knows where it is."

"So be it. I'll tell her. But, what if she can't meet then? Do you have another option?"

"Paul, let's not make this more complicated than it needs to be. If she can't make it then she'll have to tell me what's best for her. Unless she has some sort of night job that she can't get away from, she'll be there. And it is alone, isn't it?"

"Yes, that's what she wants."

"That means not you or anyone else."

"Agreed."

"Go back to sleep. I'm going to leave through the front door." He turns around but stops. "Oh, about the money, what do you have?"

Paul gives him a stare willing him to go but it does not work out that way. "My wallet has some cash, I think about fifty dollars. That's all I have now."

Damien looks around and soon spots the wallet. He walks towards it, takes all the money, about forty dollars in small bills he estimates, shrugs his shoulders without saying a word and leaves.

On his way out of the house, Damien passes by the location where Marcus is still sprawled out, not yet recovered from the booze. He steps into the room inspecting the man he loathes, thinking for a split second to do away with him right now. It could be done so quickly and simply, he thinks to himself. No one would suspect him because other than Paul and his sister there isn't anyone else who knows his whereabouts, of course, except for the man in front of him who would be dead; and dead men don't talk.

The further he considers the idea the more he likes it. Now, he only needs to figure out a way to do it. He looks around the room for something to use, such as a blunt object or a rope. There isn't anything in plain sight to use. He could use a knife. He's sure to find sharp objects in the kitchen. He remembers where they were kept when he lived here. He starts walking in that direction but suddenly stops. He has a better idea.

Why should he pull the trigger? Why not someone else do it, someone such as Paul or his sister? He likes that idea better, someone else to blame. Now of the persuasion to shift the actual deed to someone other than him, he turns to leave the room. As he passes the liquor cabinet to his left he checks out the opened bottle of DIMBLE Scotch. He hesitates for a short time before deciding to take the bottle along with a crystal glass. He leaves the house satisfied.

Chapter 8

The next morning Julien hears the devastating news of Elizabeth's death on the television. He is shocked and overcome with grief. The evil deed he put into place has backfired, killing the one he loved, not the one intended to die. He's not sure he can muster up enough energy to tell Marcus how sorry he is. He just might snap and loose control of his wits. However, if he doesn't at least pay some sort of respect there might be some suspicion, something he does not want to see happen.

The news report indicated the car was totaled with little remains to examine, yet he knows it doesn't take much real evidence to start an analysis. Since this is the second accident for the Porsche within a short time, he believes there will be some sort of investigation. He's convinced of at least that happening, and he knows he will be interviewed since he is the master mechanic. He's already figured out the answers to use.

Stranger on a Train

The real question for him now is what next to do. He decides that a visit to Varro residence is in order. He's got to keep himself together and make the visit as short as possible.

At the Varro home, Marcus, Anne, and Paul are talking. Anne seems the most upset of the trio. "I can't believe she's gone." Real tears flow from her eyes.

Marcus tries his best to comfort her but he doesn't give his daughter much support. The combination of a nasty hangover and any authentic sympathy for Elizabeth's fatality takes center stage.

Paul gives it his best but it is not nearly enough to comfort her mourning. "I'm very sorry." He can't think of anything else to say.

In fact, when someone grieves, most people don't know what to do or what to say. However, there is immediate value to many small things, such as a hug, open listening, and thoughtful words.

She lifts her head, and through her teary eyes gives Paul a smile. "Me too, I'm very sorry."

The awkwardness lasts a while until there is a knock at the front door. Marcus jumps to find out who is calling, thankful to get away, even if it is for a short distance and time. He opens the door to find Julien standing in front of him.

"Mr. Varro, I'm deeply sorry to hear about Elizabeth. I heard it on the news this morning." He is not able to use the word *death*, which is not unusual. While the d-word seems so final because it really is, acknowledging it is difficult for most people. However, accepting mortality is healthy because it actually releases the command it has over us.

"Come in," Marcus offers, hoping the new mix of people to change the mood inside the house. He is disappointed with Julien's answer.

"I think it is best your family have some quality time together. I've just come by to pay my respect and let you know you can call on me for anything." He nods his head and turns to leave, grateful he's been able to keep his presence to a minimum.

Marcus now stands alone in the doorway wishing he could either command Julien back or take his place. He really wants to check out Elizabeth's will, but knows it is best to let that happen later on. He can't appear to be too pushy on the matter, although he has nothing to hide. He wasn't responsible for his wife's car accident. He turns to reluctantly return to be with Anne and Paul who seem to be in discussion.

Now a few feet away from the young pair he decides to pour himself a drink. He moves towards the liquor cabinet. "Anyone want a drink?" He waits for a response but there isn't any, so he looks around for the bottle of DIMPLE Scotch. He can't seem to locate it so he opens the cabinet door to check inside. He only spots a new unopened bottle of the same alcohol and wonders where the opened bottle might be. Unable to come to any conclusion, he starts a fresh bottle.

"I think I'll get some fresh air. I'll be out back if you want me." He walks to the backyard without any interference from

Anne and Paul, too much engrossed in what Paul has to tell her.

Now alone, Paul says, "He came to my room last night." Before he can continue there is an interruption.

"Who?" Anne quite doesn't know who he is talking about.

"Damien."

The name sends a flutter through her body.

Paul continues. "It was late and I wasn't sure you were home or if you were I figured you were probably asleep, so I didn't consider contacting you then. Anyway, he wants to meet you by the Causeway right before you leave Sanibel. I guess there is a public beach, a small parking lot and a boat ramp on the right side. He will be there tonight at midnight. Do you know where it is?"

"Oh, yeah, I do. Tonight huh." The previous feeling lingers on.

"That's what he said. Is there a problem?"

She thinks silently. She'll have to switch shifts with another dancer, which won't be a problem. The ready made crowd who intend to watch her will have to watch someone else tonight. Any one of the girls will jump at the chance to be her substitute. They're not as popular as her but the crowd will be geared up just the same.

Next, she needs to make sure that Kyle is still on board. She's got a slight change in plans for him, but she's convinced he can be persuaded. He's got to bring with him the drug he talked with her about, the one that makes a person unconscious but in high dosages ends their life. He'll have to act fast when he meets Damien, injecting him quickly but deeply to end his life. She wonders if Kyle is physically and mentally up to it. He's got to be. There is no other way to put her brother out of her life. After he is gone then she intends to shift her attention to her father. That should be easier of the two. Paul is of no concern to her now, but later will be someone to reckon with.

When both men are gone forever, she'll spend the rest of her life traveling around the world, doing whatever she wants to do. The money she plans to inherit from her mother's will should set her up for life, at least that's what she thinks is in store for her. Or, did her mother lie about giving her the bulk of her estate? On second thought, she might want to put off the two killings until she is positively assured, but wonders when that might happen. She can't afford to be too pushy on having the will read; it might tip off the police. No, she needs to go through with the current plan.

Her inner thoughts are interrupted. He asks, "Is there a problem?"

"No, I'm just going through a lot right now. I'm adjusting."

"If this is not a good time, then we'll just call it off."

She shakes her head. "Let's do it tonight. Tell him I'll be there."

"I don't know how to get in touch with him. The deal is if you can't make it tonight he'll know it by your absence. So, I guess everything is set."

She gives him a smile without having to say a word. She has no intention of giving up any information.

Stranger on a Train

Elsewhere Julien is at his wits. He paces back and forth in his garage, still not wanting to believe the love of his life, Elizabeth, is gone. "It's my entire fault. I shouldn't have done it. I wasn't thinking." He starts rubbing his forehead feeling tension build up, wondering, rambling thoughts pass through his mind not making much sense at the moment. He takes in a deep breath and tries to settle down.

He reminisces about the times they were together, always happy, never sad. A failed marriage prior to meeting Elizabeth made him believe he needed someone to love and someone to love him. Not just anyone, but someone real special, and without a doubt not the one night stands.

He's not sure he wants to continue living without her. When night comes and he turns out the lights for bed, what will he yearn for the next day to bring? Is there anything to help him get over the pain?

An investigation of the car accident and fatality begins, but it appears the near total destruction of the vehicle makes it almost impossible to come up with a cause. The timing device is almost completely burned leaving very little evidence of its existence. However, a small fragment of coil that seems to be foreign to the Porsche's wiring system is found. That finding raises suspicion on the soundness of the initial conclusion that it was an accidental incident. The police make a call on Marcus for some help.

"I'm not the mechanic. I really don't know much about this."

The police officer recognizes a snippet of annoyance in his voice. "Who did the mechanical maintenance on the car?"

"Julien, a long time friend. He knows all about it."

"Does he have a last name?"

"Nernst."

The police officer writes the name in his notebook. "Where can I find him?"

"You don't suspect he had anything to do with this, do you?"

Not interested in answering the question he says, "I'm just looking at all angles. Where can I find him?"

"I can take you myself. Let's go, but I think you're wasting your time."

"Maybe so."

Soon Marcus and the police officer arrive at Julien's garage who is trying to stay busy working, but making little progress.

Stranger on a Train

Not paying much attention to anything right now, including the sound of the police car's engine, Julien remains under the body of a vehicle, replacing the oil and filter. He wipes sweat away from his forehead with the back of his hand. A little oil transfers to his face without his notice.

"Julien, it's me, Marcus Varro, can I have a word with you."

The sound of another person's voice surprises him, especially that of Elizabeth's husband. He wonders if the affair somehow is now public. He hesitates for a split second and then scoots out from beneath the vehicle. The wooden platform beneath his body rolls smoothly for him to see two men looking down at him. He recognizes one of them, not both.

"Hello Mr. Nernst. I'm Officer Prod of the Sanibel Police Department. I'd like to have a few words with you." All the while he checks out Julien's body movements to see if he can detect anything of importance. All he notices are the man's widened eyes, but puts that off as not being significant for the time.

Julien is not sure why Prod wants to talk with him. Yet, to be cooperative, he moves his entire body from beneath the vehicle to stand and face both men. He wipes his hands with a rag that is stuffed in a front pocket of his coverall. After clearing his voice he says, "What can I do for you."

His voice seems polite and cooperative, but Prod hears a tint of a quiver, maybe due to the surprise visit from him, a police officer. His experiences suggest that many people get nervous when talking with police personnel regardless of the subject. He'll do his best to settle the man down. "I'm sorry to interrupt your work, but I'm investigating the car accident and death of Mrs. Varro." He pauses to see if there is any reaction from Julien. He recognizes a twitch of the eye. "I understand you are the mechanic who took care of Mr. Varro's Porsche, the one that was mostly destroyed. Is that correct?"

"I maintain all the Varro vehicles."

"And the Porsche was one of them, is that correct?"

Julien takes a deep breath, "Yes, it was one of them." The less said the better he figures.

"This was the same vehicle that just a while ago had its brakes give way, is that correct?"

Marcus remains silent, not sure where the questioning is headed, but he notices some angst creeping into Julien's face.

"Yes."

"I assume you repaired the vehicle to working condition?"

"Yes."

"Quite honestly Officer Prod, I'm not sure where this is headed." Marcus buts in but is politely shrugged off.

"With all due respect, Mr. Varro, let me ask the questions. If this is too much for you then perhaps you might step outside to leave Mr. Nernst and me alone."

The admonition seems to get through to Marcus. He backs away but still in listening distance.

Officer Prod continues. "Did you find out anything about the first accident, the one where the brakes gave out, that might be somehow connected to this last one?"

Julien's face starts to get pale, something that is noticed by Prod, but can't get out the words at first. He takes another deep inhale of air to get settled down. His complexion returns to a more normal color. "No." He intends to keep from the officer anything about the tampered brakes, but is not successful.

"I understand that the brakes were altered in some way that allowed the vehicle to loose control. Is that correct?"

Julien is surprised that Prod knows this information, and his face shows it.

"I know more than what you think I do, Mr. Nernst. So, don't withhold information from me, or else I'll have you booked for obstructing an investigation. Do I make myself clear?"

Marcus feels compelled to interrupt in spite of being cautioned against it. "I asked Julien to keep quiet that information. If there is anyone to blame, then it's me."

Relieved for the temporary rescue, Julien knows he needs to be more on his toes. He can't count on Marcus to protect him for everything he's already done.

Prod turns to Marcus, "I see. I guess you and I will have a long talk after I finish here." He faces Julien. "So, what else do you know of both of the accidents?"

Julien gives Marcus a quick glance to pick up any signal on how to proceed but before he is able to read any sign, Prod interrupts.

"I'm asking you, not Mr. Varro." His voice is unyielding and serious. Then he turns to Marcus, "I don't want to tell you to leave us alone, but if this happens again, I will do just that." He waits for Julien's response, and when one is not immediate he gives a reminder, "Mr. Nernst, I'm waiting. what else do you know of both of the accidents?"

"I only know that the brakes of Mr. Varro's Porsche were tampered with. I told him that and he asked me to repair them. I also told him that I was surprised that the brakes failed because I had personally inspected the vehicle only recently and they seemed in perfect working order. He asked me not to say anything to anyone. I didn't, until now. Further, I don't know anything about Mrs. Varro's accident. I'm deeply sorry about it. She was a wonderful person." Confident that he has been convincing, he decides to stop talking for now.

Officer Prod looks over Julien one more time to detect any fishy behavior, but does not notice anything to worry him. He nods affirmatively, "Thank you. Don't go anyplace soon. I might want to talk with you again."

Julien gives a sigh of relief, now waiting to see what happens next.

"Mr. Varro, that's all I have here. I can give you a lift back to your place."

"Oh, I'll just stay here a while. There are some loose ends I've got to go over with Julien about."

Prod finds nothing irregular about the decision, so he leaves the two men alone.

Once the police officer is out of sight, Marcus says, "I'm sorry you had to be put through this." Secretly he knows he can't let Julien crack under pressure. No one can ever know about their conversation when he asked the man in front of him to get rid of his wife. He assumes Julien has not told a soul, but is unaware of Paul's knowledge. Marcus has to make sure there is no breach.

Stranger on a Train

While Julien recognizes the insincerity from Marcus, he also knows where it originates. He also inaccurately assumes they are the only ones who know of the conversation where Marcus asked him to kill Elizabeth, and he refused. Would Marcus do anything to keep that information a secret? Yet, he alone holds onto a secret that will haunt him for the rest of his life … the failed attempt to kill Marcus that led to Elizabeth's death. Julien doesn't like the place he's in, but that's reality. He must be careful. It could be a matter of life and death.

The two men stare at each other trying to read what is behind each other's eyes. Are they friends or foes, or in the end does it matter? Will each man keep his distance from the other, believing that not interfering is the best strategy? Or, will one or the other seek to gain an upper hand, to have just enough power to keep his opponent neutralized? Fear is one of the greatest drivers of human behavior. Will fear interject its might?

"I'm Ok. How are you holding up?" Julien asks, believing it to be a harmless remark.

"Fine." A one word answer is often the best choice.

Both men are feeling a little awkward right now, not sure what to say next. They turn their heads away from each other to figure it out. Julien breaks the discomfort. "I guess you need a ride home. Come on, I'll give you a lift."

The short drive is in silence.

Antonio Vianna

Later that night a scheduled meeting takes place. Everyone seems to be a bit edgy.

There is another person, uninvited, who hides behind a clump of trees nearby. Paul's heart is racing. He can't believe how nervous he feels right now. He spots someone strolling on the beach, walking into and then out of the water's waves, playing a sort of hide – and – seek game with the ebb and tide of the sea. Paul silently warns the person to turn around, to head in the opposite direction. There might be some trouble coming soon that could be avoided. No use, the silent urging is not heard.

He turns in the direction of the sound of a car's engine. A yellow Mini Cooper settles in the parking lot. He knows who the driver is. She sits inside her car, but is not alone.

"Are you sure this will work?"

"Just follow my lead. Just stand over there, behind the trees. I'll bring him over that way. Once his back is towards you, you're going to have to act fast. Inject him in the neck, or wherever gets the biggest bang. You know better than me. If he struggles, I'll kick him in the balls. That should topple him over. Then we shove him in the water. It should be over with quickly."

"You haven't paid me anything yet. When do I get paid?"

"It's all in the car. When we're done, you'll get paid." She smiles to comfort him as much as she can garner. She too feels jittery about the whole thing, but it's too late to back out. "Come on. Get in your place and be prepared."

Stranger on a Train

She stands close to her car waiting for her brother to show. She waits for about fifteen minutes, but no one shows. She wonders if maybe he finked out. No, that's not like Damien. He'll be here. Just wait a little longer.

Another ten minutes pass. She takes a glance at her watch. It's now almost half past midnight, and no Damien. She stands and starts pacing back and forth.

Approaching her is the same person previously walking in and out of the water. He carries a pair of sandals in one hand and wears a hat to partially hide his face. He moves closer to Anne. "Boo, it's the boogey man."

She jumps a little at the sound of his voice. She recognizes it as belonging to her brother.

"I thought you maybe changed your mind."

"Now why would I do that?"

She does not take him up on his question but shifts a little closer to the place where Kyle hides. He follows her lead, unaware danger is close by.

"I'm so glad you decided to come. I've missed you." She reaches to grab hold of him, to hug him in a show of sincerity, but he steps back. "I just wanted to hug you." Her voice is soft.

He doesn't trust her so he keeps his distance a little while longer. "What do you want? It's been a while."

She moves closer to trees and then positions her body such that he has to place his back towards the place where Kyle is hiding in order to face her. Every thing seems to be working just as she planned. "Can I now give my brother a little hug, please?" She waits for his response.

The action is too far away for Paul to see. He considers moving closer but decides against it, too dangerous and too probable of being spotted. He sits on the ground relinquished to being out of the loop.

She extends her arms as he walks towards her. Now touching each other, she grabs him close, firmly clenching him around her as tightly as she can, surprisingly strong. It seems like eternity before Kyle makes his move.

His movements are clumsy as he trips over a rock by his feet. He falls into Damien but without inserting the syringe.

Damien quickly turns, easily getting out of Anne's hold. Kyle falls to the earth while the syringe winds up on a pile of leaves nearby. Furry circulates through Damien's veins where the lethal injection was intended. Without much thought, he kicks Kyle in the head several times, blood seeping out into the midnight moon's light, his eyes narrowing with each blow. Anne stands by totally incapacitated to do anything, but just watch.

Damien's assault on Kyle lasts less than one minute but the effect of his thunderous blows is fatal. A smell of death from the immovable man at his feet emerges as both he and Anne look on.

Everything seems out of sync. It wasn't supposed to happen this way. Anne and Damien do not exchange glances like old married couples do, often anticipating what the other is about to say. No squabbles, no jokes, no compliments. They remain trapped in their own worlds. A squishy sound along with a trail of rich red blood oozes out of dead man's mouth.

"Jez," Damien says, unable to take his eyes off the prone body.

Anne looks away. She bends over and lets out a heave of undigested food in her stomach. She coughs. The acid taste seeps through thin spaces between her teeth. She spits out as much of the debris as possible, yet some remains caught, not yet willing to free itself.

"He's dead." The words are flat. "We've got to get rid of it." Damien behaves as if he's done this before, an experienced killer with no emotion left to care much about what happens next, yet savvy to know that the body has to disappear. "Get over here. I need some help in dragging it to the water. Let the fish have a meal." He stoops over to grab hold of Kyle's wrists. "Come on, get a move on. We've got to get this done."

Anne's gaze is still down at the sand and pebbles inches away from her pale face. She doesn't hear Damien at first.

"Hey!" He raises his voice.

The sound makes it way through the invisible brick wall between them. She blinks, and then turns towards Damien. Their eyes meet in the darkness.

Once they drag Kyle to the water's edge Damien takes over. "I've got it now." He pulls the body into deeper water and with a shove pushes it away from him. The ocean's currents do their part and soon the body disappears.

Anne continues to gaze, her eyes not focused on anything in particular, as Damien walks past her.

"Let's get out of here." He heads towards the parking lot. Out of the corner of his eye he spots something on the ground just about where he was attacked. He leans over to pick up the syringe and then sees a small black bag. He takes it as well. With Anne trailing behind him he opens the bag where he finds two glass cylinders with some sort of wording he doesn't understand. He stops to read the small print but the moon's light is not strong enough for him to see.

By now Anne is along his side. Her voice is hoarse from vomiting, too painful to say anything. She knows exactly what Damien is holding, but knows better than to admit anything.

"Some sort of junkie," he says still looking at the items.

She takes a step ahead of him to avoid a conversation right now. She's got to figure out quickly what her next move is. She reaches her Mini Cooper ahead of him and fumbles to get her keys out of a pocket. They fall on the ground.

By now, he's caught up with her. "I'll get them. You're all shook up."

Thankful for a little more time to regain composure she waits for him to hand her the keys.

"Let's get in. You drive someplace away from here. We've got to talk."

She wonders how much of a tale she can dream up before she has to say something. She's not sure how much he'll believe, but to tell the truth right now is simply out of the question. A little acting along the way is in order.

Still too far away to know what exactly happened, Paul decides to leave, mistakenly thinking that Anne or Damien will fill him in on the details.

During the silent drive he sees something in her face that he had not expected. Not fear. He's seen that before in enough people to recognize it. There is something else he isn't quite sure. He feels an itch that he can't seem to scratch, but he's convinced he'll find it.

Out of the corner of her eye she sees him staring at her, inspecting her to figure out what she may be thinking, feeling, or planning to do. She has to control herself to hide the truth. There is very little she hates more than when someone can figure her out. She's got to make it look good. If not she might find herself in company with Kyle. The mere thought sends a flurry of shivers through her body.

Now on Periwinkle Way headed toward Captiva Island he breaks the silence. "Where are we headed?"

"Near Blind Pass Beach. Great for shelling."

"I didn't bring a pail."

"Don't worry. I've got it covered." She's relieved the little banter is working. Hearing her own voice along with his settles her nerves. It is amazing how their gibberish makes sense to them after all the years being apart from each other.

He checks out the interior of the car. "Nice wheels." He sees a bag in the back seat, but pays no attention to it. Why should he? There is twelve hundred dollars in small bills that was intended for Kyle once he finished the job. Too bad he'll never see it.

"I like the color." Self confidence is building rapidly and now she is ready. "I'm glad you came. It's been a while."

He shrugs his shoulders, not interested in rebuilding a sister – brother relationship that was not that strong to begin with. He knows she's up to something.

"Who do you think that guy was back there?"

"Not a friend of mine. What do you think?"

It is her turn to shrug her shoulders. She challenges him to be on the offense. "What's in the black bag?"

The bag rests on his knees. "A couple of glass cylinders that's filled with something. I also found a needle on the ground that he was planning to stick me with."

"What do you make of it?"

"I don't know, maybe a junkie who was spaced out."

"And we were at the wrong place at the wrong time."

"Seems that way."

Each suspect the other is playing a cat and mouse game; but who is the cat and who is the mouse, or does it really matter?

At the corner of Periwinkle Way and Dixie Beach Blvd. is the *Heart of the Island Shops*, a good place to park the car this time of night. She turns right into the dirt parking lot.

"Let's talk," she says.

"Ok, you wanted to see me." He moves his body to face her.

"You've always liked getting right to the point, so here it is." She is convinced the story she is about to tell is believable. "Mother is dead."

"I know. Is that why you wanted to talk with me?"

While surprised to realize he is aware, she goes on. "Do you know who killed her?"

"I heard it was a car accident."

"Do you believe that?"

"It seems you don't."

"I think it was father."

"Why?"

"Come on. We both know they weren't really in love. You knew that when you lived at home. Give me a break." She thinks she's loosing control of the conversation.

"Most people fall out of love but stay together for convenience. Come on, give me a break."

"There marriage was different. You know that."

"Where is this all headed?"

"Whether he actually killed her or was only responsible for her death, he's never been a good husband for mother or a good father to us … including Edna. It is time for him to leave us permanently."

"What do you propose? I'm all ears."

"We've got to find a way to get rid of him."

"Kill him?"

"If that's what it takes."

"And who do you recommend do it?"

"Together, we must do it."

"You're real serious about this, aren't you?"

"Quite serious." Her eyes narrow as she tightens her fingers into clenched fists.

His eyebrows lift and he feels his hands tighten around the handles of the black bag still in his lap.

"I think I've just come up with a way to get him." She loosens the muscles in her hand sensing he has bitten the bait. "Let's see what you've got in that bag."

He frowns at first and then takes a peek again. He pulls out the syringe and then one of the two vials. He hands over to her the small container containing some sort of liquid.

She already knows what's in the container, but acts as if she is inspecting it for the first time. With a serious look on her face she reads aloud the information on the label. "Propofol. Short acting intravenous sedative agent for use as a general anesthesia for adults and children. Warning: a lethal side effect is propofol infusion syndrome with high dosages; also dystonia leading to involuntary muscle spasms. Do not use if patient uses alcohol or has high blood pressure. Consult your physician for further possible toxic effects." She pauses to exaggerate her next point. "Eureka. I think we found an accomplice." She lifts her eyebrows and with a half-smile stares at Damien. She waits for him to catch on.

His lips turn upward. "An interesting coincidence."

"What are you saying?"

"Please, give me a break."

"There are lots of things I don't understand, but I do understand chance. Call it luck or fate, or even call it coincidence. We have something right here, right before us. Are you going to turn away from it?"

"I don't trust you."

She gives him another fake frown. "What have I ever done to you?"

"That's it, I don't know."

She considers giving him a good old fashion pout, but doesn't think that will work with him. He's too hardened.

He goes on, "Maybe you should do it yourself. You don't need me."

Stranger on a Train

She knows he's right about that, but has no intention to do it alone. "I just thought you'd like to divvy up the work, you know, like a partnership."

"If you want a partner, get Paul, your lover boy, to be it."

"He's not my type."

"Really?"

"Really, and he doesn't have the stomach for it."

"It seems like you don't have the stomach either."

"What do you mean?"

"Back there. Didn't you heave out your guts?"

"Ok, I'm a little squeamish around blood."

He thinks she is through but is mistaken.

"Mother's will gives me most of the inheritance. Father gets a little, just enough to live well below his current life style. The rest goes to charity. You don't get anything, but I can cut you in on my part. We can live in the house together, or do whatever you want separately. You can be truly independent. You can even get back into playing the piano, if that's what you want. Anything! Doesn't that sound great?"

He lets it all settle in. While he still distrusts her, it just might work out. He is tempted to agree. "How do you know about the will?"

"She told me about it."

"Does he know?" Damien has a difficult time recognizing Marcus as his father.

"No."

"He's going to go ballistic when he finds out."

"To put it mildly."

"When do you think he'll find out?"

"I heard him talk with the executor of the will yesterday. She's coming over tomorrow to give us the details."

He gives out a smirk, "I'd love to be there."

"Oh, I can arrange that."

He gives her a quizzical look at first, but then after realizing what he said he understands her answer.

"Do you want to see him fly off the handle?"

"I want to think about it."

She is persistent. "Think about what? What further information do you need? Let's be honest, Damien. You're not in a bright stage of your life. I have no idea where you're living, but I suspect it's not someplace you want to stay forever. I'm giving you an opportunity to take a big leap into something better, something that we both agree you deserve. It's owed you for all the pain you've been through. All you need to do is partner with me on this one thing. I think I know exactly how to do it. Do you want to hear?" She suspects it is now just a matter of reeling him in.

He knows she's up to something, probably at his expense. She's not changed a bit since they were children, usually blaming him when she got into trouble. Still, he is curious about what she's schemed up with. He agrees to just listen, nothing more. "Ok, what is the plan?"

Without any hesitation, she tells him. "He's been drinking heavily the past few months. I often see him passed out on the couch. The house hasn't changed much since you left, so you probably remember his liquor cabinet and the big sofa and chairs." She does not wait for his acknowledgement. "Once he's out, he's really out. All you need to do is inject him with

228

this stuff, maybe use both containers. No one will suspect. It's fool proof. We can do it. I know we can. I can get you into the house without anyone knowing."

She takes a chance by grabbing his arm, hoping the touch will seal the deal.

"I'm in. But I want to witness his reaction when the executor reads the will."

She is jubilant, but resists showing off too much. A gentle smile and a little squeeze in the same place on his arm are sufficient for now. "I know a place where you can hide to overhear everything."

Hidden in a nearby closet close enough to hear the conversation among the executor of his mother's will, his father and sister, Damien patiently sits. With no free flowing air to cool off the temperature he begins to sweat. It begins to feel as if he is in a cage. He estimates only ten or fifteen minutes have passed, but he is unsure. He wipes off the perspiration from his eyes with the palms of his hands. To pass whatever remaining time he has cooped up he thinks about being free from his father, and to have real money to spend, not stealing and coning with every chance he gets. He likes the image he conjures up. Inner thoughts are interrupted by some commotion. He refocuses to listen in.

Antonio Vianna

Feet stepping on the wooden floor signal people walking nearby. The sounds are muffled so he strains to hear exactly what is said, pressing his ear against the door. He makes out most of the conversation.

"That's preposterous!" Marcus shouts. "She wouldn't cut me out. She loved me."

"Mrs. Varro has not cut you out entirely. You can live in this house, free, as long as you are alive and as long as Anne agrees to it. You keep your Porsche, and you receive fifty five hundred dollars, gross, per month. You'll of course have to pay Federal income taxes on that monthly amount, but nothing to the State of Florida."

"That's pittance! I can't live on that! The Porsche is destroyed! Are you sure you are interpreting the will accurately?"

Anne remains silent, delighting in the formal announcement. She suspects Damien is also tickled.

"Yes I am. It's all here clearly spelled out. You can read it." She extends the document for his perusal but he refuses, waving his hand to shove it away.

He stands to get a drink, pouring a double Scotch, and downing it in two gulps. It gives him a wallop. He staggers a bit before regaining balance. Turning to Anne he asks, "Did you know anything about this?"

"No father. It's as much of a surprise to me as it is to you. But please be assured you can live here as long as you wish. That's a promise." Her voice is soft and sincere making Marcus more irritable.

He mumbles an assortment of profane words beneath his breath, his face reddening as fast as the anger is building. "I want to challenge it!"

"Excuse me?"

"I said I want to challenge it, the legality of the will. It might be a forgery. Elizabeth might not have been of sound mind when she wrote it. I want it challenged!"

"That's quite unusual, Mr. Varro."

"So be it!" he shouts back, his anger is furious and almost out of control.

"You will have to hire an attorney on your own. They can be expensive."

"So help me, I'll do it! She's not going to screw with me!" He takes in a deep breath. "And you, young lady, will not control my life! You can count on it!" He storms out of the room.

The executor remains silent, yet her face tells it all, surprised. Silently she looks at Anne to say something.

"I understand him. He's offended, and I suspect still grieving over my mother's death. I'm not sure I would be any different. I think he'll get over it."

"You're a remarkably understanding daughter. He should be thankful."

Anne gives one of her best saintly smiles she knows how. "Is there anything I need to do, paperwork to sign, or whatever?"

"Yes there is. Sign where I've marked with a checkmark and date it today." The executor points to three places on the document. "I need your father to sign as well, but it might not be the right time to ask him."

Anne signs and dates where asked all along saying, "I can take care of that. Can you leave it with me?"

"I wish I could, but there needs to be a witness from the court, like me, when he signs it."

"So what does that mean?" She wonders if implementing her part of the will is going to be delayed.

"It means he cannot receive anything until he signs. Your part, since it was signed in my presence as a witness, is complete. I'll mail you an official copy of everything as soon as I officially file this. While all of your inheritance takes affect immediately, you won't be receiving your monthly checks for another thirty to sixty days. It takes that much time to establish the payment process. Can you live Ok until then?"

"No problem."

"Fine. That's all I have to do. I can show myself out." She packs up and walks away.

Now alone except for Damien in the closet, she whispers to her brother. "It's safe to come out."

He enters the room, his shirt soaked in sweat and his face a little weakened from the heat. "What a show?"

"Him or me?"

He chuckles, "I guess both."

"What's next?" He begins to feel more confident in his sister's ways, which also means he needs to be on the look out should she turn on him.

Anne hears another set of foot steps from another room. "Go back in the closet. Someone is coming."

Stranger on a Train

Damien makes his way behind the doors just in the nick of time before Paul enters the room.

"Hi. I just passed your father outside in the front yard. He didn't seem pleased with something. Is he alright?"

"Oh, he'll get over it … just a little disappointment with his part of the inheritance." She wants to let out a big grin but resists. No sense in letting on to him, no value in it at all.

"Was that the executor who I saw just leave the house?"

"Yes."

He waits for more information but nothing is forthcoming, so he changes the subject. "How did your visit with Damien go last night?" He intends to keep from her his undercover antics, although he didn't see or hear much.

"It went very well. We agreed to see each other."

"Fantastic. When?"

"Soon."

Again, Paul hopes to hear more but is disappointed when she keeps quiet. "I see."

She says to herself, "You have no idea."

He feels a little awkward right now as if he just ate the last piece of cake that was set aside for someone else. "Ok, then, I'll just leave you be." He turns and walks away. His instincts kick in. Something is not right but he can't seem to get a hold of what it might be. The pieces are just not falling into place.

Without needing a prompt from Anne this time, Damien steps out of the closet. They begin making plans for later on tonight.

Antonio Vianna

Just as expected, Marcus returns, headed directly to the liquor cabinet. He rubs the stubble on his chin considering he might grow a beard. He wonders why that thought flashed through his mind. Now settled down a little, his reddened cheeks have returned to a more normal color, yet he's still angry as hell. The thought of Anne inheriting a vast majority of his wife's wealth pisses him off. He's bound and determined to correct the injustice, as he sees it.

There were many times he wanted to leave Elizabeth, but for good reason stayed put. Just from the practicality of economics, he could never make it on his own. He needed her in spite of the loss love between them. He wonders how it all started, if there might have been some critical event early in their relationship that he should have picked up on. Nothing comes to mind at the present. Running off would have been his death sentence, in a way, but staying here has become one as well. Should he just live out the rest of his life under the terms and conditions dealt him?

After he and Elizabeth decided on separate sleeping room, there were times when he would suddenly wake up feeling a presence of someone, or perhaps of some thing, he was never totally sure. The sensation startled him so much that he thought he was going insane, yet never sought professional help or talked with anyone about it. His skin would get tingly like something was crawling inside his skin. Scratching it away was no use; it only served to heighten his worry.

Afraid to turn on a light or call out for help he sought another means to feel safe; a .44 mm handgun fully loaded that he kept in the top drawer of a nightstand close to his bed. The feeling of being watched while he slept was creepy and it frightened him.

On few occasions he thought he actually saw a figure at the foot of his bed but was never really sure. The same with an occasional sound that he convinced himself was like a human cry for help. Those were times of real increased heart rate; he clenched his chest on those occasions thinking he was experiencing a heart attack.

Nothing has changed much, except an increased appetite for booze. It seems to take the edge off his nerves and peacefully put him into a slumber like mood to rest. He pours a hefty shot of DIMBLE Scotch in a glass and slowly walks to take a seat in his favorite chair. Slowly he sips the liquid.

A few minutes later, he hears a knocking at the front door. He ignores it, not wanting the alcohol induced pleasure to vanish. The knocking continues, so he begrudgingly gets up to find out who the caller is.

Julien stands on the other side of the door's entry way. "Mr. Varro, can I have a word with you?"

"Can't it wait? I'm rather busy right now."

"It should only take a minute. It's very important."

Annoyed at himself for accommodating Julien's request, Marcus says, "Sure, follow me. I'll pour you a drink." There is no mistake about his resentment.

Settled in facing chairs, Marcus asks, "What's so important?"

At first Julien doesn't speak, his fingers clenched around the chair's armrests. For a second it seems that he has changed his mind, to reconsider the sensibility of the visit by saying something innocuous and then leave him alone. There are no whispering words of wisdom to help him out; his brain seems to have shut down.

Marcus, however, shows his impatience. "What is so important? Tell me."

Something clicks in his head. He blurts out, "I was in love with Elizabeth." There is something in his voice that makes it sound true, yet not at first to Marcus.

"Yes, yes, we all loved her." He passes it off as nothing more than a comforting remark. "Is that what's so important?" He looks ahead, yet, at the same time he sees something else in Julien's face. He hesitates to ask, however, too interested in ending the unasked for visit and conversation.

With the ball back in Julien's court he has to decide what to do. He rubs his sweaty palms on the chair's armrests, feeling itchy all of a sudden. Humdrum thoughts pass through his mind, too afraid to think of the more important ones. He opens his mouth to say something, but as quickly closes it racking up annoyance points with Marcus.

"This is the most unusual conversation I've ever had. What is it you want to tell me? Come out with it, or else, find your own way out of my house."

"Elizabeth and I were lovers. It was only a matter of time before she left you." Julien undergoes both a sense of relief and one of discomfort at the same time, if having opposing feelings simultaneously is at all possible. The wait to hear Marcus seems endless.

He feels an emotional rage looming within himself, getting up enough steam to blow up. He throws down the remains of scotch and without hesitation refreshes the drink. Now with his back turned to Julien, who anxiously sits waiting what might come his way next, Marcus says in a composed manner, "Get out of my house, and never come back." Is this the calm before the storm?

Not realizing when to cut his losses Julien tries to explain. "We were soul mates who ..."

With the force of a full blown typhoon, Marcus starts to rant and rave. "You come into my house after my wife dies to tell me you've been screwing her! I don't believe a word of it. You are a very sick man ... no ... you're the devil spreading its wickedness ... making the innocent like my wife, appear to be evil. Get out and I hope you rot in hell!" He flings the glass with all its contents at Julien. It hits him in the forehead, cutting the skin just above his left eye. "Get out!"

Julien touches his head feeling the place of contact. He suddenly feels ill; his tongue is dry, and his skin is clammy. He knows there is nothing he can say, so he leaves the room not realizing Anne and Damien have witnessed everything from a short distance away.

Not feeling much of anything right now Marcus automatically pours another drink in a fresh glass. He is intent to get as drunk as he can, the best he can hope for right now. It doesn't take him long to pass out.

As soon as they think it is safe Anne and Damien walk close to Marcus. She nods, "Do it." She steps back to let Damien inject the toxic drug.

Damien shoves the needle into the side of Marcus's neck, introducing Propofol into his blood stream. He yanks the needle out once he finishes, and looks somberly at the man who is about to die.

While still passed out from the scotch, his body jerks as the drug makes it way through the proper channels. It doesn't take long before Marcus is dead.

Anne steps forward to be by the side of her brother, "Well done. I'm proud of you."

"He deserved more. He should have suffered. I'm sorry he was too drunk to feel the pain."

Suddenly, there is a noise in the background. They hear the front door open. There is no knock. Steps advance their way. Quickly they retreat to find a secure hiding place.

Julien returns. He walks into the room intent to say something to Marcus but stops when he sees the man slumped in a chair. He steps forward but before he can get too close, a crashing blow hits him on the back of his head. He topples to the floor. Anne looks on still holding a fireplace iron shovel. "This is perfect," she grins in a sinister way.

Damien isn't sure what she means but follows her orders just the same.

"Wipe off the syringe with something. Make sure your fingerprints are gone from it. Then place the syringe in his right hand as if he did the injection. I'll wait a few hours before contacting the police. You've got to leave for now. I'll take care of the rest. I'll say that I found Julien injecting father with something but it was too late for me to stop him. The only thing I could think of doing was to hit him on the head with something." She pauses for a second, "How does that sound?"

"I like it. Also say that they were arguing over something, but you couldn't understand exactly what it was."

"Good, that's real good. You have to leave here. How can I contact you?"

"That's difficult. I'll contact you in a few days."

"Ok, now go."

Damien leaves Anne alone. She waits a few hours before making contact with the police.

Her story is convincing to the authorities and Julien is arrested on suspicion of murdering Marcus in spite of his explanation of what really happened. Additionally, upon further investigation, he becomes a person of interest in the death of Elizabeth and the earlier attempted murders of Marcus and Paul in the Porsche. He has no defense to these suspicions, so he keeps silent.

Chapter 9

A few days pass as Damien keeps hidden and Paul plans to return to Carlsbad. Both aims are interrupted.

"What are you doing?"

"Packing. There's no reason for me to stay here."

"Oh, but what about me?"

Paul looks up, briefly suspending filling his suit case with clothes. "I don't follow you."

"I thought that we could get more acquainted with each other. I mean, while it is sad that my parents are dead, I'm in this big old house alone."

"You've always got your brother. By the way, where is he? I thought you two were going to get together."

"In due time. I think he's got some things to work out."

The arch of his back goes from pleasure to pain as Paul straightens up. He winces a little.

"I can help that." She flickers her eyes seductively.

There was a time, just a little while ago, when he'd give his heart and soul to her sexual advances. Not now. He's a little bit wiser and much more careful, or so he thinks. He's still not prepared for what she's got in store for him.

She comes closer to him.

For a second she thought he was going to say something or back away. He remains put.

She starts working her mojo. She moves her face close to his, brushing her cheek against the side of his face, nipping slightly on his ear. Her left hand slowly creeps up his back until it reaches the nape of his neck where she cradles him. Now she whispers words in his ear that excite him. Gently she blows sweet air. With her other hand she reaches between his legs to find his most sensitive spot. Slowly and carefully she turns him on. "I want you."

As much as his mind tells him to resist, he cannot. He takes her with all his might.

Even if he tried to remember what happened next, he could not, maybe because he really doesn't want to reconcile the polarities that exist within him; maybe there are other reasons. What he does know is the full and complete pleasure of being with her, the sense that she is the only important person or thing in his life right now. He might even exclaim that he'd do anything for her, whatever the price, whatever the cost. He belongs to her, and that sounds wonderful to his ears. But he should be careful what he wishes. It just might happen.

"Kiss me. Touch me. Don't let me go."

Paul decides to stay one more week just enough time to get Anne and Damien together, to mend their family ways. Anne suggests he might be their counselor of sorts, to help facilitate working out any problems. With seemingly nothing to lose, Paul agrees. "How do we contact Damien?"

"He'll either contact me or just show up. Either way, the ball is in his court."

As if on cue, there is a knock on the door. Anne and Paul look towards the sound at the same time. "I'll get it," Paul offers.

Standing before him is Damien, holding a bouquet of flowers. He appears neatly dressed and in good shape, unlike in previous times. "Hi Paul, I'd like to see Anne."

There isn't much of a greeting exchanged between the two men. Paul feels a little clumsy for some reason. He doesn't know why. "Good to see you." Paul steps aside. "I think you know the way, straight ahead." He closes the door and follows Damien.

Now seated, the trio remains quiet, not sure who is supposed to begin. Paul starts it off. "This is nice, the three of us together." He realizes the inept beginning almost immediately.

"I'm so happy you're here, Damien. I hope we can become close, as sister and brother."

"Me too. Here … some flowers for you."

While this has all been rehearsed before, it is so well performed that Paul has no idea there have been practices to perfect it. He decides something on the spur of the moment.

"Maybe I'll let you two get more comfortable with each other. I'll just take a walk around the house and be back in an hour or so. How does that sound?"

Anne and Damien give each other a glance, "Ok, sounds like a good idea."

Paul leaves the sister and brother alone. He does not realize they are fine tuning his ultimate fate, but he will soon find out.

"Are you ready?" she asks her brother.

"Ready as I'll ever be."

They wait until Paul returns. As soon as he enters the room, the action starts. He doesn't have time to duck. The punch is thrown so fast and efficiently it catches Paul square in the nose. He falls over.

After he left his family, Damien grew up fast, fighting fast. He already had the physical strength beyond most boys his age. However, living on his own from day to day added to his potency. When compared to Paul who neither developed the muscle nor had the right experiences there isn't an even match.

Damien quickly jumps on him and starts pounding him with punches one after another. He seems out of control. If the beating doesn't end soon, Paul will surely be dead. But, that's not going to happen if Anne has her way.

She changes the agreement with Damien on the spot and smacks him with a firewood iron poker. He tumbles to the floor, surprised at the turn of events. He doesn't know what's going on. The sharp crack sends a howl from his mouth, and then a lot of blood. The red liquid seeps on the floor forming a circular puddle. The two men on the ground are now separated, although neither moves.

She moves to Paul and feels his pulse. While not very strong, he is still alive. She glances towards Damien who remains still for the time being. She leaves both men to rush towards the kitchen for a glass of water to give Paul. Upon returning Paul has moved a little and shows signs of recovering. His lazy looking eyes stare at her. She gives him a smile, "Everything is going to be alright. Just take it easy."

He tries to say something, but the words don't come out clearly enough to understand.

"Don't try to say anything. Be quiet." Her voice is reassuring to Paul as his breathing starts to get back to normal.

At the same time Damien starts to move ever so slightly. His fingers try to scratch the floor surface but without making any marks, too weak to do much of anything. He slumps back without further movement.

Double-crossing Damien is her only way to save herself, but that means having to deal with Paul, the lesser of two opponents she figures at the present time; easier to get rid of Paul later on than to deal with Damien by himself. She is placing her entire future on that decision. Is it a long shot or a sure bet?

She's got to move fast to finalize the part dealing with Damien, so she lets go of Paul telling him to rest for a while. "I'll be right back." She places the glass of water on the floor to his side.

He doesn't recognize much of anything going on right now.

Stranger on a Train

She checks Damien's condition, satisfied he's not about to move. Then, she pours into a glass tumbler a full glass of scotch and brings it to him. She pulls out the second vial of Propofol that she kept hidden and opens the top. Cradling Damien's head she opens his mouth and begins pouring the toxic agent into it. At first it goes down easily, but then he starts coughing. Some of the liquid spreads to her blouse. "Be careful." She grimaces to offset the words. She continues the process until the entire vial of liquid is gone.

She returns the empty vial to her pocket and plans to dispose of the evidence later on. Next she starts feeding him scotch. This step takes a little longer as he more frequently spits up the fluid. She reminds herself to burn her clothes. Once the entire glass of scotch is emptied, she lets his head touch the floor. She wipes the glass of her finger prints the best she can and then hands it over to him making sure his finger prints are the only ones on the tumbler.

She returns to check out Paul for a short time. He's now out cold.

She's got enough time to drag Damien someplace to hide him, tie his hands and feet, cover his mouth and nose with tape, and then get back to Paul before he knows what's going on.

She returns to comfort Paul. It takes about a half hour before Paul is cognizant of anything.

"What happened?"

Pleased he doesn't remember much, she explains to him what he needs to know. "Everything was going just fine at first. Then, he went to the liquor cabinet to pour himself a drink.

He gulped the first one so fast, as if he'd never had anything so good; then a second one, and then a third. I told him to slow down, but his eyes got red. I'd never seen anyone like that before. I felt afraid for my life." She pauses knowing all along he's buying the story. "Then you returned and he came after you. I don't know what came over him. All I could do was to react without thinking. I hit him on the head as hard as I could. He fell to the floor. Then you started to come around. I came by your side, where I belong." She runs her fingers through his hair, giving him a warm and pleasing smile that soothes him. "How are you feeling?"

"Uhh." If he could be anyplace else he'd go there at the drop of a hat. He grabs his sides but they're too sensitive to his touch. "Ouch."

"I guess you're in pain."

Dah! His expression tells it all, so he doesn't respond.

"He's gone." While not a total lie, the implication is Damien has left the building. He hasn't, he's just someplace else, stuffed in a closet, tied and gagged. By now he's surely dead or darn close to it. The change of plan is working out just fine with her. There's more to come. "Just rest in my arms. I'll take care of you."

There's not much more he is capable of doing at the moment, so he closes his eyes. Soon he is asleep, but dreams of strange things.

Love and hate are opposing forces.
Some say that love is stronger than hate.
Others believe just the opposite.
Whatever the truth, they are compelling.

246

Stranger on a Train

He opens his eyes.
He is not sure where he is.
He blinks a few times.
Now he knows.
He's never been here before.
Things smell differently.
The odor is much stronger than ever before.
He takes in a deep inhale.
He shuts his eyes to keep away the truth.
His hands and face feel different.
They are course and hairy.
He touches his cheeks.
His heart's increased beating is not fake.
He looks at his hands and inspects his feet.
He is shocked.
They are paws, full of fur and claws.
What has he become, and why?
His feels his body change.
It goes from frigid cold to burning hot.
The animal nature is now part of him.
It takes control.
He has turned.
Now on all four legs he lifts his head.
He sniffs the air again.
He senses some thing nearby.
He takes in another whiff.
To his left are two wolves.
One is prone on the ground.
It is defenseless appearing.
This one appears to be male.
There are wounds on its neck and torso.
Blood is oozing out.

Antonio Vianna

The other, with a stretched neck, gnarls.
Jagged teeth show.
Bits of animal flesh cling to it.
This one seems to be female.
She takes one last swipe.
Its sharp claws make a final tear.
The weakened male wolf shrieks.
The move ends its opponent's life.
A short whimper is barely heard.
Its head drops to the ground.
She looks around to spot him.
They glare at each other, mouths open wide.
They sound off, warning the other of danger.
She begins with the first attack.
She is much stronger than he imagined.
She bites him on the neck.
His blood tastes good to her.
She wants more.
He doesn't want to give her anything else.
He manages to pull her face away.
One of his claws swipes her shoulder.
She doesn't seem concerned.
She comes at him again.
This time he is ready.
His mouth is wide open, teeth positioned.
At exactly the right moment he acts.

The limit of Anne's patience is the degree to which she finds value in it. She carefully lets Paul's body rest on the floor as she readies herself for the final chapter of her plan. She's quite convinced that she's got Paul exactly where she wants him, and in just a matter of days she'll be free from those who have information to implicate her. She leaves him alone for the time being.

Finished changing clothes she burns them, and then continues to clean up any remaining incriminating evidence. She wanders to her father's room and gets the .44 mm gun. She has plans to use it later on. It's been about forty-five minutes since she left Paul. She checks in to see how he's doing.

She finds him sitting upright, leaning against the wall. The color in his face seems improved so she takes a spot next to him. "You're looking better. Think you can stand?"

She seems on his side, at least that's what Paul thinks. "Yeah. Give me a hand."

They move to another part of the house where it is more comfortable. She has a few things to tell him. "Let's get out of here for a few days. We both need a break."

He returns her smile with one of his own. "Sure, but aren't you going to report what happened here to the police?"

She's not dumb but right now is a good time to act like it. "What do you mean?"

"What I mean is Damien tried to kill you and me. I'd consider that important enough to report it to the police."

"Do you really think the cops will find him?"

"That's not the only point."

"So clue me in."

"You have to report these kinds of incidences so they have on record what happened. It becomes part of his police file and can be used when he commits another crime. I think he's dangerous. I think you need to report it."

"Hmm, I see." She continues the con. "Why don't we get out of here for a little bit to let our heads clear, and then when we return we go to the police?"

While he's not keen on the idea of waiting, he gives in. He figures he needs her more than she needs him. "Ok."

Her enthusiasm heightens. "I know of the perfect place."

She drives her yellow Mini Cooper. Getting to J. N. "Ding" Darling National Wildlife Refuge is easy. It is difficult to get lost. She takes Periwinkle Way until it dead ends on Tarpon Bay Road. Then, she turns right on Tarpon Bay Road for only a short distance. Signs to the Refuge are clearly marked straight ahead.

With a good understanding of the tide charts, she knows the times for high tide and low tide, sunrise and moonset. She feels confident knowing how this will all end. Their conversation is odds and ends of stuff that has little importance to her except to keep him engaged in their relationship. He's got to trust her or else her plan won't work.

In a short time they find the canoe launch site where they rent a two – person canoe. They launch it in Tarpon Bay. It seems a perfect place for Anne's plan to work. She carries a bag that contains among many items the .44 mm revolver.

"Ever canoed before?" she asks.

"No." He moves his arms through the straps of the life preserver that she'll try to remove once they get a good distance from land.

"Ok, then. Take the fore and I'll take the aft." Seeing his frown she realizes he doesn't understand. "You take the front seat and I'll take the rear one. I can steer us back here."

"Oh, Ok."

She mimics putting on her life preserver.

They are now far enough away from shore and headed towards some mangroves. The sun's rays start beating down on them. "Want some water?" She pulls out from her bag a plastic bottle of water.

"Yes, I'm thirsty. It's sure warm on the water."

She reaches forward to tap his shoulder with the bottle. She takes one for herself.

He turns slightly to grab it. He opens it and takes a long swallow.

She takes a sip from her opened bottle as well. Then, she determines it is time.

"Why don't you lean back on me, rest your head in my lap, close your eyes, and think of dreamy things. Maybe even me." The words are spontaneous, yet the plan is well thought out. She removes the life preserver but sets it close by, and then takes off her top exposing her breasts.

He leans back unaware of what's going on.

"Ah."

Antonio Vianna

"What's wrong?" He straightens up and looks back. He is surprised but not unhappy at what he sees. "My oh my." It's all he can say.

"You approve?" She gives him a wide grin, inviting him to push the envelop.

"What do you think?"

"I think you like what you see, and want some of it. Do you?" While her smile is still wide, he is focused on something else.

"Yes." He isn't sure how to take the next step, something she's already planned on.

"Take off your life preserver, then your shirt. Then, if you're really a good boy, I'll let you in on all of it. I'll take off my shorts so you can enjoy everything."

He makes his move as quickly as he can and soon he is ready to have her. He's turned his body to face her.

"I think you forgot something."

He frowns but follows her eyes. "Oh." He removes his pants and briefs. Once they are both totally naked he advances her way.

She lets him enjoy her sweetness for a short time, but not too long. She has more immediate things on her mind. Just when she thinks it's the right time, she grabs hold of the revolver. She gives out a few more moans and groans to keep him interested so she can be fully prepared. "Ooh, this is too much. Stop, you're driving me crazy."

He is not deterred, almost out of control with pleasure.

She is persistent as she shoves his head away from between her legs.

Stranger on a Train

He looks up to see the revolver pointed directly at him.

"This is not easy. I was beginning to like you, I mean really like you, in spite of you being a writer." The words are flat and her eyes convey the same lack of emotion.

Suddenly he sees his entire life flash before him. He is not supposed to die this way. In fact he is not yet ready to die, but does not know how to get out of it.

There is a clicking sound but no explosion. There is nothing as frustrating than when a gun jams.

This is his only chance. He flips to his left side into the water.

The canoe capsizes tossing Anne and the boat's contents overboard. She looses her grip on the gun. It sinks to the water's muddy bottom eventually out of sight. She reaches for a life preserver that is nearby, clinging to it, all along reprimanding herself for the sloppy work. She looks around for Paul, but can't spot him, now even more determined to put him away. Eventually she grabs hold of her shorts and halter top that linger on the water's surface. At least she has something to wear.

Paul, on the other hand, while he is safely away from Anne, is without clothes. To him, that's the least of his worries, but still a concern. He's got to get something to wear and then try to understand why Anne wanted to kill him. He waits some distance away but still in eye sight of the upside down canoe.

She tries to reset the long narrow boat to its upright position but is not strong enough, so she swims to shore to report the incident, albeit without all the details.

Antonio Vianna

Paul sees Anne move away from the boat and figures it is a good time to get closer to it. Maybe he can find something to wear; at least that's what he hopes for. He does a half – somersault dive at the waist hoping to find his shirt and shorts. He lucks out and surfaces with both items in hand. He returns to shore to figure what next to do.

Anne sees two other canoes within shouting distance, so she gives out a yell for help. They respond to her call, amazed at her story.

"Paul, the man who was with me in the canoe, went berserk after I told him that I wanted to put off our marriage a little while longer. I said I only needed a little more time to think about it, one of the biggest commitments a woman could make. You understand, don't you?" She looks at the two other women facing her, while for the time being avoids face contact with the two men.

The women nod their heads in agreement.

Anne goes on. "I thought this was the guy I loved, but now I'm not sure. He had a gun and was prepared to use it on me." She gives all four a look of fright that hits them square in the eyes. "The only thing I could think of was to jump overboard. I didn't know what else to do."

She forces a few tears from her eyes. "Then I swam away as fast as I could. I have no idea where Paul is, even if he is alive, because he too went overboard. He is dangerous."

One of the female canoeists says, "You've got to report the incident to the police."

Stranger on a Train

The other woman agrees with a nod, while the two men remain quiet. The men have doubts about her story, but can't quite put their finger on it.

"I probably should, but well, I don't want him to get into any more trouble."

One female tries to explain. "Listen, this guy almost killed you. He's dangerous. You said it yourself. If this happened to me, you can bet your britches I'll report it."

The two men roll their eyes.

"Can you take me back to the main entrance? I should tell them about their canoe. I think it's sunk."

Elsewhere Paul dresses in his wet clothes and makes his way towards the parking lot. He sees Anne's yellow Mini Cooper and wonders what he should do next. He spots something that might be what he needs. He sets out to rent a bicycle.

While his wallet is soaking wet, the credit cards are useable. He pulls one out to use.

Disregarding the rules to remain within the confines of the Refuge, he bikes to 2763518 West Gulf Drive, hoping to make it there before Anne. All the time he thinks of a plan to settle it all. He knows he is up against a strong willed and evil person. He hopes he's up to the task. He has to be, or else he will not see another day. He peddles faster, not concerned about obeying any traffic laws.

When he safely arrives at the destination point, he should be out of breath and tired, yet the adrenalin pumping through his body more than compensates for it all. He takes the bike to the side of the house to make it inconspicuous to Anne when she arrives. His plan all depends on surprise.

Thankful that the front door is unlocked he moves fast to set up the scheme. However, he is temporarily distracted when he smells a strange odor coming from someplace deeper in the house. Curious, he checks it out to find Damien's dead body stuffed in a closet, taped and bound. The sight is ghastly. Paul leaps back in repulsion. Nausea starts to set in and he gives out a heave, throwing up what little is in his stomach.

He decides to use Damien as part of his plan, so he drags the dead body towards a chair located about fifteen feet from the front door's entrance, close by the stairs leading to the second floor. He is surprised how heavy a dead body feels. It is more than he had expected to handle, but he rallies enough energy to complete the task.

He sets the body upright, needing a broom stick to insert down his back, between his shirt and bare skin. Otherwise, the body is too limp. He removes the tape around his face and nose, and cuts the rope that ties his hands and feet. He finds some extra materials in the closet that were probably left behind by Anne to secure Damien's body in the chair. Finally, he turns the chair so that Damien's back is to the front door.

As fast as he can, Paul moves to the stairs, pounding on each step to find which ones are unstable. After moving up six stairs he finds two consecutive steps that serve his purpose. He looks around for something to loosen the steps further. The iron poker from the fireplace does the trick.

Next, he takes some of the remaining rope to string between each side of the railing of the stairs. He places it just so that it lays unnoticed on the wood until he is ready to suddenly tighten it. Anne should easily trip.

He weakens the railing at this place making it quite unstable.

He turns off the master electrical switch for the house preventing anything electrical to function.

Thinking he is done, another idea pops into his head. He speedily moves a stand with two candles in holders next to the chair and body. He finds matches near the fireplace to light the candles. They flicker nicely, but will even be more eerie when the room darkens in a while.

Satisfied he waits for Anne to return. He hears her car pull up within twenty minutes. He listens carefully although his pounding heart competes for his attention.

The front door opens. It is quiet, deadly silent.

Paul sees her carefully walk towards Damien and then stop just a few feet away.

She lets out a scream realizing who is sitting before her. Her fright lasts but a short time, now realizing a trap has been set for her. She turns away from the body. "Nice piece of work, Paul. Come out come out wherever you are. It won't work. I've reported you to the police. You can't hide."

He stays put. She won't intimidate him anymore. He gives out a holler, but she doesn't react the way he expected she would. Maybe she didn't hear him, or maybe she doesn't care?

She turns around not sure where the sound is coming from.

He repeats the yell with the same reaction from her. Next he throws a few shells on the stairs. They tap their way down a few steps, surprising Anne.

She jumps.

Paul is pleased.

She slowly moves towards the steps not sure of the sound.

Paul tosses a few more shells towards the front door just when she is about to take a first step up the stairs.

She jumps again and so pleases Paul.

"You're not that clever." She tries to upset him but is not successful. For the first time in a while she feels on the defense, something she does not like. Yet she is resolute about not losing.

She lifts her foot to walk up the stairs. One step at a time is what she figures she needs to do. Now on the third step silence remains.

"Just three more," Paul whispers to himself not expecting her to answer.

She helps him out with advancing two steps quickly.

Paul needs to time his next action almost perfectly. He reaches for another few shells and readies his throw at the candles hoping to create enough confusion on Anne's part to upset her balance.

Stranger on a Train

She does her part as she makes it to the sixth step. It wobbles as she tries to hold onto the railing.

In quick succession, Paul throws the shells towards the two candles, pulls the rope taut, and gives out a holler. The shells knock the candles off the stand.

Anne flinches as she shifts her body to the right. She topples down the stairs falling on her left arm. Her head hits the floor with a thump. She does not move.

Paul thinks it's all over, once and for all. While he should feel some sort of sorrow for what's happened to her, he doesn't. Has he become like her? He hopes not. He steps closer to Anne, to inspect what he believes to be a dead body. He's now had more experiences in a short time with dead people; he should recognize it when he sees it. Yet when he looks into her still open eyes, he's not sure. There seems to be some life lingering deep within. It frightens him to think she might still be alive.

He steps back to get a hold of himself. What should he do next? There is Damien, surely dead, sitting in a chair just a few feet away, and Anne, at his feet, not moving at all. Will the police believe his story? What story should he tell? Should he contact the police at all? Maybe he should just leave this place to return home, his home, in Carlsbad, California? He's not sure what to do. He steps outside in the darkness to clear his thinking. A full moon shines overhead and the stars wink towards earth. The air smells sweet.

A guilty conscience takes over. He decides to drive to the Sanibel Police Station to tell his story. He's not sure they'll believe him fully, but to run away would surely throw blame on him. He'll take his chances.

It's just a short drive before he parks his car in front of a small building identified as Sanibel Police, Main Headquarters. He wonders if there are other locations throughout the Island. Paul hesitates, reconsidering whether to go through with it all. He's come too far to back out, so he goes inside. Officer Prod is on duty.

Paul steps forward. His appearance is less than credible looking, dried and wrinkled shorts and shirt, rumpled hair, and barefooted. "I'm Paul Autore, and I want to report some deaths at the Varro residence." He remains standing in front of Prod waiting for some instruction to tell him what to do next.

Prod frowns. He's seen a lot of crazy things in his life, but this one is close to the top. However, upon hearing the name of Varro, he takes it more serious. "Sit down. What do you have to say?" He leans back in a worn wooden leather chair. It squeaks when he shifts his body.

"This is going to sound very strange, but you have to believe me." He does his best in chronicling the events between Damien's attack on him and the death of Anne. He is not interrupted as Prod tries to piece together his sense of what might have happened.

"Hmm."

Paul is not sure what to make of it, so he waits to hear more.

"Let's take a drive to the Varro place where the two bodies are alleged to be."

Stranger on a Train

"You don't believe me, do you?"

"Mr. Autore, let's be honest. You don't look particularly credible in the way you're dressed. Second, this all seems to be over the top. Know what I mean? But, I'm willing to go along. All we need to do is check out the house."

Figuring this is the best offer he's going to get, he agrees. They drive to the Varro residence.

Paul reaches the front door first and tries to open the door. He wiggles with the door handle a few times but it doesn't seem to respond. He frowns.

"Maybe it's locked."

"It shouldn't be. I didn't lock it when I left."

Officer Prod wiggles his eyebrows and leans toward the door. He knocks twice with the knuckles of his right hand.

"No one is going to answer. I've already told you that they're dead." Paul's voice is close to a whine combined with a little desperation mixed in.

Seconds later they hear a clicking sound as the lock's mechanism is released. The door opens. Standing before them is Anne, dressed in a nightgown. She squints her eyes and gives out a yawn. "Yes?" She seems totally confused to see the two men. "What is it?"

Paul does not know what to say. There does not seem to be any abrasions on her face, where she fell, and definitely she is not dead, but quite alive. He takes a deep swallow and starts to get uneasy.

"Sorry to bother you, Ms. Varro, but Mr. Autore says there are two dead people in your house, you being one of them. I'm just following through."

Antonio Vianna

"Dead people in this house?" She seems genuinely surprised. "Would you care to look around?"

"I don't think that will be necessary. I'm sorry to bother you. Good night." Officer Prod turns to Paul, "Satisfied?" He pauses, "Let's go. I'll drive you back to the Station where you left your car."

Paul continues looking at Anne, flabbergasted. He doesn't know what to make of it. "No, let's go inside. Maybe she isn't dead, but I know Damien is." He steps forward to enter but is held back by Prod.

"I don't think you want to make more of a fool of yourself than you've already done. Let's go and leave Ms. Varro alone."

Paul is persistent, "No, this can't be true. I know what I saw."

"It's alright Officer Prod. Let Paul inspect the place. He won't find any dead bodies here. I've actually been worried about him for the past few days. He's been acting strangely."

"Oh, how so?" Prod's curiosity is heightened.

"I think it's all about some sort of fantasy he has with me, teasing and embarrassing me."

"Do you feel threatened in any way?"

"Oh, no. I can take care of myself. Really I can."

Paul listens in disbelief. He wants to shout down her lies but it's really her word against his, and so far, his word hasn't exactly been right on. He decides to cut his losses and leave Florida as quickly as possible. "Let's go." He walks away.

"You'll be coming back here, won't you Paul?" Anne asks.

Stranger on a Train

He whispers underneath his breadth, "Not on your life."

Epilogue

A month later Paul is busy with work, finishing off the final revision of his newest novel. There are moments when he flashes back to the stay in Florida, but for the most part he tries to put aside that part of his life.

He hears the engine of the white mail delivery truck stop. Without looking up he knows Fred Booth, the U. S. Postal Carrier, is about to fulfill his routine daily work. He smiles to himself and goes back to the final touches of his manuscript.

Unexpectedly, his doorbell rings. He moves in that direction to find Fred Booth handing him a special delivery letter, postmarked Sanibel Island, Florida. He stares at it

"Got to sign for it."

"Huh."

"Sign right here," Fred says pointing to a specific place.

Paul finishes his part and quickly is left alone holding onto the white envelope. He waits a few seconds as if he is expecting awful news, but he has no idea what's inside. Slowly, he unseals the envelope, breathing starting to accelerate.

Cash tumbles out, hundred and fifty dollar bills. There is a one way airfare ticket that falls to the ground. A silver crucifix is taped to the letter. He starts to read it.

Stranger on a Train

My dearest Paul:

I've missed you since you left. Why did you abandon me? I wish you would return to be with me. I feel so isolated in this big house.

Enclosed is the remaining fee promised you by my father. Also is a one way airline ticket to Ft. Myers. I can meet you at the Airport.

You brought out the vampire in me; something that I knew existed but did not want to accept. I fear others are not safe with me, except you, only you. Life together can be forever. I can assure you of this, but you will have to trust me.

The silver crucifix is my promise to you. Wear it always.

Your eternal lover,
Anne

He tries to breathe easily, but has a difficult time taking in the air almost gasping as if he had held his breath under water too long. In staring at the religious object, he feels powerful, protected from all evils.

Is trouble looming?

He scratches the left side of his neck that's been pestering him since his return from Florida. He hasn't yet noticed the two small punctures.

Antonio Vianna

He feels something overtake him that he can't explain.
Can he make sense out of it or should he just wait to see what
happens?

He kisses the crucifix.

- end -

Antonio F. Vianna

Antonio F. Vianna holds a B. S. Degree in Biology from Union College (Schenectady, New York), a M. M. from Northwestern University (Evanston, Illinois), and is a former Officer in the United States Air Force. He is frequently on television and radio offering practical tips for taking charge of your career, and is available for speaking engagements, and ghost writing projects. Mr. Vianna is on-faculty with multiple universities teaching graduate level and undergraduate level business, management, leadership and human resource courses; he also conducts workshops on "Re-Careering at any Age," and "How to Write a Book and Get Published." He lives in Carlsbad, California. His books are available almost everywhere. His website is http://www.viannabooks4u.com. He is one of our most prolific writers in both fiction and non-fiction. Published books with AuthorHouse include:

FICTION

A Tale from a Ghost Dance (2003)
(ISBN: 1-4107-1384-9)

The In-ter-view (2003)
(ISBN: 1-4107-0876-4)

Talking Rain (2004)
(ISBN: 1-4140-6648-1)

Uncovered Secrets (2005)
(ISBN: 1-4208-1795-7)

Midnight Blue (2005)
(ISBN: 1-4208-6397-5)

Veil of Ignorance (2006)
(ISBN: 1-4259-1695-3)

Yellow Moon (2006)
(ISBN: 1-4259-5112-0)

Hidden Dangers (2007)
(ISBN: 978-1-4259-9710-6)

Haunted Memories (2007)
(ISBN: 978-1-4343-2852-6)

Bound and Determined (2008)
(ISBN: 978-1-4343-7450-9)

NON-FICTION

Career Management and Employee Portfolio Tool Kit
Workbook, 2nd edition. (2005)
(ISBN: 1-4107-1100-5)

Leader Champions: Secrets of Success (2004)
(ISBN: 1-4184-3684-4)

Made in United States
Orlando, FL
03 June 2022

18463689R00167